Sons of the Black Hand

by
Carolyn Kvajic

PublishAmerica
Baltimore

First printing

ISBN: 1-4137-2051-X
PUBLISHED BY PUBLISHAMERICA, LLLP
www.publishamerica.com
Baltimore

Printed in the United States of America

Dedication

Where did all the love go?
This novel is dedicated to peace.

Acknowledgments

To my wonderful husband, Philippe, who put up with my obsessive needs to put this story on paper. To my loving family, both Croatian and Serbian, who were enlightened enough to move beyond the strangleholds of the past. And, finally, to all those who die every day in the name of peace. May this world deserve your sacrifice.

CHAPTER ONE
GOSPEL

*"Once the game is over, the king and the pawn
go back in the same box."*
Italian Proverb

"Auf Widersehen, mein Freund," Joseph whispered, crossing himself as he bent over the closed coffin of his friend and mentor of fifty years, a man who had taken with him so many shared memories and so many promises of a future they would now no longer share. At five minutes to nine in the morning, the temperature hovered at ninety degrees in the shade and the wind was as still as death when Joseph left the funeral parlor, emerging into another sweltering South Florida day.

Pulling off his tie and undoing the top button of his neatly pressed, white cotton shirt, Joseph realized why so many of the Cuban men in the area wore *guayaberas*, the short-sleeved, linen shirts that had recently become a fashion staple in Miami. It was like going against a law of nature to wear anything more in this sizzling, tropical heat so different from the cold climate he had once endured. The thought caused him to feel chilled for a long moment as he remembered all the others, friends who, like Fritz, he would never see again.

This was Joseph's second funeral in under a week and he stared wearily at the few mourners gathered outside the chapel exchanging condolences and business cards, some fanning themselves with the printed obituary notice they had been handed when they had entered the chapel an hour before. He knew them all, some better than others, but he had no inclination to engage any one of them in conversation. Too much was happening too soon and he sensed danger in the air. Not here, perhaps. Not now. But coming soon. He was certain of that.

Wandering away to a corner of the courtyard, he leaned against the hibiscus-covered wall, nervously twisting the ring that he wore on the third finger of his left hand, a massive ornamental band set with a bloodstone, a gem known as the martyr's jewel. According to legend, the bloodstone was created from the blood of Christ which fell from the cross and stained the jasper at his feet, forever branding the stone with the color of suffering and sacrifice. Only centuries later was the stone's face etched with the seal of a carved eagle, clutching the Iron Cross, all in deference to the fraternity. It was this stone that reminded Joseph that the seven men who wore it were bound together by the blood ties of a brotherhood which could never be challenged except, as had happened to two of them already, by sudden death.

Beads of sweat dropped onto Joseph's white linen jacket as his already small eyes narrowed yet further and his nostrils flared like those of a stallion anticipating battle.

The enemy has reared its ugly head again.

Suddenly lightheaded, he leaned against the wall and tried to catch his breath as he watched a cluster of brown fig leaves blow across the red terracotta tiles and into the art deco fountain that stood beneath an umbrella of fronds formed by four royal palm trees. The leaves floated like dead soldiers on top of the water.

The funeral had brought back memories that had taken him far from this exotic setting. As the priest had chanted a liturgy over Fritz's casket earlier, Joseph had been reminded of April 1945 when the invading Allies had finally closed the doors of Jasenovac, one of the most barbaric death camps. Joseph knew that his days were numbered now but he was determined not to end up like Fritz in a mahogany coffin, his face blasted beyond recognition. No one deserved that. No one. Staring up at the cloudless sky, he said a silent prayer for the dying.

"Not a bad turnout, after all," someone said in a deep voice.

Joseph's heart skipped a beat as he turned to find Wilhelm Heidrich, his friend and the benefactor of his University of Miami's endowed chair. For over fifteen years, Joseph had been given *carte blanche* as chairman of the Political Science Department, thanks to Wilhelm's influence over the dean of Arts and Science, as well as the university's president, an influence which was dictated by his friend's annual six figure donation. Thanks to him, Joseph had the leisure to conduct his own research, write scholarly papers and collect awards. And, thanks to Joseph, Wilhelm was living the life he might have lost.

"You're late," Joseph said nervously. "The service is over."

"My plane was stuck on the runway," Wilhelm told him, running his fingers through glistening, thick gray hair.

"Well, at least you made it to *this* funeral," Joseph said sharply. Despite the debts they owed to one another, there was always a tension between them. Perhaps, he thought now, they shared too many memories.

"There aren't that many of us left," Wilhelm said in a low voice, removing his sunglasses. His eyes, as always, reminded Joseph of a shark's, watchful and yet, somehow opaque. At any rate, it was impossible to see the man behind them.

Drawing Joseph down on one of the iron benches that dotted the courtyard, Wilhelm reached into the top pocket of his black silk Hugo Boss jacket to pull out two Hoyo de Monterrey Double Corona cigars. As the pungent, oak-scented smoke rose around them, the bearers passed, carrying the coffin.

"Here's to you, Fritz," they said in unison and then, as the hearse doors closed, Joseph added, "What do we do now?"

"First we need to see Fritz buried," Wilhelm said, throwing the cigar on the ground and grinding it out with the heel of his shoe. "Then we will make our plans. Come along, *mein Freund*. Let's not desert him now."

Once they were in the limo that was waiting, Joseph let his head fall wearily against the headrest. "I can't believe they're dead," he muttered. "Both in one week."

"I warned them," Wilhelm told him, pressing the button to close the glass partition between them and the driver as they headed north on Biscayne Boulevard. He poured two shots of brandy from a silver flask. "They could be on a beach in Mexico right now if they had listened to me."

"*Bitte*, Wilhelm. Don't start. Not today," Joseph said as he stared out the window at the morning sunlight reflecting off the glass sheeted high-rises that lined the bay. Built during the heyday of the drug cartels, most of this real estate was, he knew, funded by money launderers and drug kingpins, many of them men who sat on local bank boards to this day. Al Capone and the Mafia might have made Chicago, but it had been a motley crew of Cuban émigrés and cocaine cowboys who had put Miami on the international map again.

"The police tell me that a Fed-Ex package exploded in Fritz's hands," Wilhelm said, drinking his brandy in one gulp. "Apparently he told his secretary that it was a doctoral thesis he was supposed to review, something about Arab-Israeli relations in the 21st century. Then, when he opened it …"

"I guess tenure isn't what it used to be," Joseph said sadly, reaching for his glass.

"Knock it off with your bullshit American cavalier attitude, will you?" Wilhelm's eyes narrowed. "I'm here to keep you from being a fool like the others. Just remember this, Joseph. *Nie sich ergeben.* Never surrender. Never show fear."

For a moment, the two aging men sat silent, lost in their own private worlds.

"We will protect you, just as we always have, *mein general*," Wilhelm said finally. "These rings will bind us forever. But you know that we have to act now, don't you. We can't wait any longer. There's too much at stake."

Joseph did not answer him until they were standing with the other mourners at the graveside.

"*Es macht*," he finally said in a low voice as the coffin was lowered into the ground. "Go ahead then. Do it. It's time to call the Brotherhood."

CHAPTER TWO
LIE IN THE DARK

"I've developed a new philosophy ...
I only dread one day at a time."
Charlie Brown

A blast of U2 rock music shocked Alex from her drunken stupor. *And, I still haven't found what I'm looking for ...* Reaching for the nearest projectile, she aimed an empty Evian bottle at the clock across the room. A direct hit. Damn, she had impeccable aim even with an aching hangover. A few more precious moments in that quasi-state of sleep was all she longed for. But no such luck. Any chance of continuing the slumber was rudely shattered as she tasted the dregs of bay oysters, Tabasco Sauce and key lime pie. The events of the night before suddenly crystalized in her mind.

"What time is it," murmured a voice from beneath the mound of her paisley Laura Ashley, goose down comforter. Sitting up abruptly, Alex quickly realized she was not alone.

"It's time for you to get your delectable ass out of my bed and out of here," Alex ordered with an air of defiance.

A tanned muscular arm reached for her, pinning her down across her torso.

"Ummm, come over here, baby."

Jason's deep voice was hoarse from smoking too many cigarettes and singing backup vocal accompaniment to the Red Hot Chili Peppers' *The Righteous & the Wicked*. He had wailed the chorus over and over, until they passed out at 3:00 AM, an early night by South Beach standards.

A feeling of claustrophobia overwhelmed Alex as the song reverberated in her head like a malfunctioning CD player electronically stuck on a single verse. Her long, silver bejeweled fingers caressed Jason's forearm. Carefully planning her attack, she clamped down on a clump of blond hairs and yanked as if she were plucking feathers off a dead fowl.

"Shit, what'd you have to do that for?" growled her injured paramour, retracting his burly forearm. "You are one piece of work, Alex."

Rising from the bed, Alex threw open the Venetian blinds. A bright stream of sunlight cruelly penetrated their dark cocoon, highlighting the remains of their nocturnal sojourn. The room was a mess. A half-empty bottle of Ketel One vodka sat prominently on her rustic Indonesian night stand next to an ashtray overflowing with Marlboro Lights cigarette butts. A line of clothing littered the bedroom floor, revealing the progress of a night of seduction. Alex picked up a black teddy with her toes, flinging the garment into her right hand and twirling it on her long index finger in quick 360-degree motions.

Nursing his injured arm and squinting like a bat ambushed by daylight, Jason curled himself into a fetal position. "Damn girl," he shouted. "You are such a maniac!"

Alex returned to the edge of the king-size bed and bent down to look straight into his chiseled face. "At least you're never bored," she whispered with satisfaction, stroking a baby fine lock of hair from his hazel eyes before dropping the teddy on his face and heading for the bathroom, smiling.

God, he wanted her. He felt a surge of passion rise between his legs as he thought of caressing her long, tanned body. He rose, rubbing his bloodshot eyes, and slowly followed behind.

Alex's naked body gave him a permanent hard-on. He could stay hard after hours of making love, wanting her over and over again. Yet, she was still a stranger after all these years. Some people you never get to know.

"Hey, babe, how about Thai food tonight?" he asked playfully, mimicking chopsticks with his index and forefinger.

"Sorry, Jason. I have plans," Alex told him dismissively, grabbing a tube of Crest.

"You always have plans," he said, walking up behind her and yanking the toothpaste out of Alex's hand. He twisted her to face him. "You know a relationship is about give and take and all you do is take."

"Sorry, but I just don't have time to process your need to feel wanted right now," replied Alex, her eyes bright and wild in an instant. She stood naked, glaring, challenging Jason to a confrontation he knew he couldn't win.

"I hate you sometimes," murmured Jason as he tossed the toothpaste into the sink and stumbled back into the bedroom, throwing on his Levi's 501s. "I'm outta here!" he muttered, grabbing Alex's last pack of cigarettes as revenge.

"Don't you dare!" Alex said sharply.

Seeing the fury in her jet black eyes, he quickly tossed the cigarettes back on the bed.

"Hormones, baby, hormones! Get those puppies under control!" Jason wailed as he stormed out the door half dressed, his Hawaiian shirt in one hand, Reeboks in the other, on the way to his brand new, 1992 white Mazda Miata.

Alex smiled, imagining Jason's 6′2″ frame fitting into that Japanese clown car. As much as she teased and tortured him, she knew he was salt of the earth, God blessing his kind, Midwestern soul with patience and generosity of heart. At the end of the day, a gem in the rough was better than a litter of one night stands.

She reached for the pack of cigarettes, lit one and inhaled deeply.

At least he understood that she was not part of this world. Occasionally she was sweet and tender but only at night, right before she fell into a restless sleep, otherwise she was what Jason called "a rip-roaring nightmare of a beautiful woman."

In Alex's universe, war and love were waged in similar fashion. Both were chaotic and fierce yet passionate and enduring at the same time. And, both were nurtured by a breath of fire. Jason's singed edges were evidence of that.

Alex felt a tinge of loneliness as she stood at the bedroom window and watched as he peeled out of her driveway. She was comforted though, knowing full well he'd be back, nuzzling her neck and cooing words of love in a couple of days. And, she was making progress. This was only the fifth time in under a month that Jason stormed out of her apartment fuming. Alex headed for the shower, aiming the cigarette into the toilet.

As steam interred her in a sheath of moisture, she grabbed a towel and wiped at the dank mirror, staring as her reflection appeared. Dark circles framed Alex's heavy, crestfallen eyes. Her life was ruled by ugly demons, haunting her with their distorted voices, echoing, promising to fill the inexplicable void with false nourishment. They beckoned her. All she had to do was give in to their seduction. But not today. She had a job to do.

The day's agenda was full. As a general reporter, Alex was sent her to cover all the mundane community events, and today's assignment included reporting on a condo association meeting for the local section of *The Miami Gazette*.

That morning the Deco House condo association was holding a vote on a no children policy for the complex. One of the residents had become pregnant at the age of fifty-five and the retirement community was unhappy about the prospect of baby pee in the pool.

As a graduate of Northwestern University's prestigious journalism program, she had dreams of investigating earth-shattering events, stories that moved nations and toppled presidencies. But no, her article *du jour* would get four inches of space on page five of the Local Section of the paper— "Postmenopausal Grandmother to Birth New Tenant in Geriatric Facility." This was Pulitzer Prize material?

Dripping wet, Alex stomped back into her bedroom, glancing at her answering machine. Shit, she hadn't checked her messages last night! War, assassinations, nuclear disaster, an emergency school board meeting— anything could have happened since she sneaked out of the office at three yesterday. The world was moving at rocket pace while she drowned her sorrow in martinis. Anything to numb the pain.

"*Chiquita, escuche me,*" Jose Martinez, Senior Editor of *The Miami Gazette,* bellowed. "You haven't answered my pages and your story sucks! I'll save your ass this time but you're walking on a thin line, *mi amor!*" An ominous dial tone echoed in her ears as he hung up on her machine.

"Shit!"

Alex lit another cigarette and rushed back to the bathroom to apply her makeup. Gotta look good in this town. There were too many eighteen-year-old leggy models roaming the landscape and you had to compete. This day called for Chanel Red. She checked herself out in the mirror. Alex was healthy, athletic yet elegant in a casual way. Not bad for a twenty-eight-year-old—not a bit of cellulite, legs to her neck and perky tits. Plus she had a brain. Too bad that wasn't a desirable commodity in this town of brainless, beautiful wonders!

Her sour mood faded as she thought of Jose managing his staff of newsroom misfits. It was like herding cats. Some were young and ambitious, most were alcoholics and none were controllable. But Jose's skillful guidance produced some of the best reporting this side of Alligator Alley.

As one of the youngest reporters, she adhered to a pecking order, struggling to write stories that deservedly belonged in the trash, and this was going to be one of them. She grabbed her knapsack and headed out the door, dressed in white linen pants, a light blue camisole and blazer. Stepping out into the brilliant morning was like opening the door to a steam bath. Another hot, humid day in Miami. What else was new? She cursed her aching head as she drove her 1968 convertible Mustang east on 395 towards the Atlantic Ocean and South Beach.

Early morning on South Beach resembled a patchwork of cultures loosely joined by frayed thread. School kids clothed in grunge wear shared bus benches with blue-haired mavens and *Marielitos* waiting transport to their daily labor. At Wolfie's restaurant, a 1950s relic reminiscent of Miami Beach glamour days, cackling Jewish matrons shared counter space with handsome, gay lads fondling nipple rings.

The sun, broad as a Cheshire cat, smiled down on the newly raked beaches, groomed for another day of nude sunbathing. Local Cuban merchants opened storefronts filled with cheap electronics, beckoning visitors with Latin Muzak. Mom and pop thrift shops narrowly carved out a living, selling *tchotchkes* in a neighborhood invaded by Gianni Versace, Guess and funky haute couture boutiques.

South Beach was unlike any other place on earth. Known as America's riviera, the Art Deco district was stylish, eccentric and ultimately trendy. The most in-vogue of in-vogue destinations, the fifteen-block radius transported visitors to the 30s and 40s but spiced it all up with electrifying neon lights, sleek and sexy interior designs and eye-catching, pastel colors.

Alex left the chic district behind as she drove up Collins Avenue towards the Deco House, a monstrous beachfront condo conversion on 17th street and tossed a "PRESS" sign on her dashboard. She parked in the loading zone.

The lime-green lobby was overflowing with aging patrons drinking Folgers coffee and congregating by a table laden with bagels, lox, cream cheese, and pastries.

Alex crimped her nose as she was struck by the smell of mothballs and urine, a consistent welcoming mat in most geriatric residences. The smell of approaching death won the battle against cheap over-the-counter perfumes sprayed generously to mask the internal decay.

She roamed among the crowd, eavesdropping on tales of aching joints, lethargic bowel movements and negligent children.

"So, he slept with a prostitute. Does that mean he can't be a competent city commissioner?" queried a fragile old man.

His attempt to engage his companion in political dialogue was met only by a dazed look.

"They don't have the prune danish today," responded his friend, looking as though he might break into tears as he searched for the pastry of choice. His frail body, thin as silk, shook as he finally settled for a jelly donut. He was just one of many of life's warrior saints, left to muddle in his memories.

The brightly-lit lobby resembled a bizarre carnival, known to locals as God's waiting room. An old woman, paraded about the lobby in a pink striped leotard and high heels, proudly displaying her protruding, wrinkled belly. Newly coiffed elderly women emerged from the hair salon, their hairdressers having struggled to add volume to sparse locks. War paint applied to brittle, yellowed nails at weekly manicure and pedicure appointments masked severe calcium deficiencies. As much as they tried, they couldn't escape the indignities of old age.

Alex surveyed the flamingo pink lobby, absorbing ambient details for her article. Another day, another dull story. Then she noticed him.

His tall, lean body commanded the room—a warrior god exacting worship from his followers. A few strands of his wavy black hair hung loosely about his long, angular face, escaping the constraints of his tight ponytail, as his broad, muscular shoulders invited the world to place its heaviest burdens upon him. He was King Alexander reincarnated as a Calvin Klein model. His sculpted Slavic cheekbones framed eyes large as saucers and black as Apache tears. Staring at a face so much like her own, Alex felt as though she were paralyzed.

Moving with the elegance of a panther, his body was in perfect symmetry as he turned and headed for the exit to the pool.

Their eyes met. Deep and mysterious, his gaze transfixed her for a brief moment before he turned and exited through the automatic sliding glass doors. Alex followed. Stumbling into the bright sunlight, she saw him facing the Atlantic, letting the breeze blow against his taut, athletic body. The tall stranger turned and faced her like an ancient fighter—defiant, proud and generous of spirit, spreading his arms much like a phoenix emerging from the ashes for his flight to glory.

"*Za krst casni i slobodu zlatnu!*" he bellowed, invoking King Lazarus and his noble fighters to bless him with their courage and piety.

Suddenly, an explosion rocked the condominium complex, blasting concrete slabs and faux art deco fixtures into the air. Thick black smoke escaped the building. Glass cascaded down like vicious snowflakes as the forty-foot oceanfront window shattered into millions of deadly projectiles.

Alex quickly rolled to her side, her Aikido days feeding her natural tumble and she sought refuge against an overturned banquet table.

Crab-crawling across the floor like a marine dodging bullets in a barrage of enemy fire, Alex scrambled toward her knapsack and cellular phone. Was this Cuba's revenge for the Bay of Pigs thirty years later, she wondered. Whatever it was, it was front page news.

Alex stumbled to the railing and looked below to where the stranger had been standing, but he was gone. Slowly she staggered back into the building, battling a wave of nausea. A warm trickle of blood flowed down her forehead.

An otherworldly silence filled the lobby for a few disorienting seconds, then groans and wails could be heard from beneath the debris. A cloud of dust hung above the destruction, forming a gray layer. It was surreal.

Eyes stinging and lungs heaving for fresh air, Alex doused a pink napkin in the overflowing fountain water and covered her mouth and nose before turning and heading for the gaping hole that was once the sliding glass door to the building, stumbling over the broken concrete and overturned furniture, praying that those below the debris were still alive.

Once outside, Alex rushed past the firemen on their way into the building, and sat on the sidewalk across the street, staring at the smoke billowing out of the second floor. She quickly dialed Jose's number at the newspaper from her cell phone.

"Jose, it's me," she said, coughing uncontrollably.

"Goddammit—Alex, where the hell have you been?" the senior editor yelled. "I've been trying to contact you since yesterday. You disappear one more time like this and you're fired!"

For a moment Alex couldn't respond. Smoke had filled her lungs.

"I knew it! You're hung over again. I can't keep covering your ass. By the sound of it, you're not even in your usual ornery state to give me some lame excuse."

"Jose. I'm at the Deco House," Alex gasped, her voice the barest croak. "There's been an explosion."

"*Mi hija,*" he said, suddenly changing his tone from drill sergeant to concerned parent. "Are you alright?"

"Yes, I'm okay but I saw someone right before the blast," Alex explained, watching as police cordoned off the premises with yellow tape to prevent the crowd from blocking the entrance to the rescue workers. "Jose, I have a stinking suspicion that this was deliberate," she said quietly, as goosebumps rose on her bare arms.

"*Jesus Cristo!*" Jose muttered.

"You're not kidding. I'll need more than the *Father's Son* to help me out with this one," Alex told him, trembling in earnest.

"What do you need from me?" asked Jose, after a beat.

"Leave room on page one," said Alex, a determined edge in her voice. "You'll have the story for the late edition."

CHAPTER THREE
BRETHREN REBORN

"Peace, like charity, begins at home."
Franklin D. Roosevelt

Miami's hospitals handled gunshot wounds and bizarre third world diseases on a daily basis, turning emergency rooms into top training grounds for triage students and disease specialists. Casualties of the explosion only added to the burden of the emergency response teams. Many of the injured were airlifted, although most were transported by ambulance to Mount Sinai, Jackson Memorial and Cedars of Lebanon, suffering from lacerations, burns, broken bones and severe smoke inhalation. Alex was the last patient admitted and the first to be discharged.

The hospital staff rushed to process Alex's paperwork as a gang of reporters sat waiting for the young journalist in the hospital's conference room.

Her first front-page byline appeared in the late edition of *The Miami Gazette*, sandwiched between a story on the US President throwing up in the lap of the Japanese premier and the United Nations deploying troops to Croatia. The President's upchuck, apparently in revenge for the trade imbalance, sent the Nikkei into a tailspin, while the UN brokered cease-fire between the Croatian government and the Serb rebels landed some 14,000 peacekeeping troops in Croatia. Alex's story was in good company.

According to Police Chief Eduardo Lopez, a leak of liquid petroleum gas had probably caused the blast in the geriatric facility, smashing windows and storefronts all along Collins Avenue for two blocks.

The 10:35 AM explosion in the congested district ripped a fifty-foot-wide hole in the concrete building, partially collapsing the second floor and exposing rooms. Authorities said it was a miracle more weren't killed.

Two residents, Hans and Zelda Gottsfried, had complained about gas leaks for weeks. The blast originated in the couple's kitchen in apartment 203, killing both of them instantly. Authorities said Hans was a retired Stanford University professor.

As Alex entered the conference room, a television reporter clamoured, "How does it feel to have survived?" The normally unfazed Alex blushed a crimson red, as she walked towards the podium table and sat down, pulling the mike closer to her mouth.

After clearing her throat, she replied in an almost inaudible tone, "I have a bit of a headache, but I was just doing my job."

Alex moved away from the mike and sat smiling sheepishly, realizing that she sounded like a rookie fullback, post Orange Bowl victory. If she didn't immediately get a grip, she'd soon be staring into the television cameras and thanking her mother and God for her good fortune. Maybe it was all the painkillers the nursing staff gave her during her brief hospital stay that rendered her capable of nothing more than spewing unoriginal sound bites. In any event, Alex wasn't prepared for the onslaught of questions and beaming camera lights. She shuffled uncomfortably in her chair.

"This is a big break for a young reporter. What's this going to do for your career?" hammered a stringer from one of the weekly news magazines. He smirked as he elbowed another journalist standing next to him.

Alex just smiled and squinted her eyes as she stared at the room full of her colleagues. Then her mind began to drift. She knew journalism was a cut throat business, and just because she was one of their own didn't give her immunity from their assaults.

On any given day, reporters circled like vultures, waiting to pounce on a visible carcass, surviving on the misfortunes of others, feasting on dead or decaying matter. Their tenacity resulted in what most called "news," but few deemed in the public interest. And like the birds of prey, these so-called members of the Fifth Estate waited impatiently for their daily meal.

Kidnappings, crimes of passion and child killings were as abundant as the "green shoe" syndrome present in most South Florida closets. The furry growth, fond of leather left unused in dark places, multiplied with a vengeance, much like the crime rate on a hot, humid day. Miami was a petrie dish of human frailty, and horror stories oozed out of every nook and cranny, hiding in hot shadows, awaiting discovery.

"Ms. Miletic, are you alright?" interrupted a reporter from the local public radio station. "You look a bit green."

Shaking the cobwebs from her brain, Alex responded, "Sorry. Yes, I'm fine. Like I said, I'm just glad I made it out alive and I had an opportunity to file the story," retorted Alex. "I feel for the people who were killed and wounded. I've been very fortunate," she added, breathing in deeply as the room began to spin.

Jose Martinez, Senior Editor of *The Miami Gazette*, interrupted the onset of questions, concerned about his main gal. "That'll be all for now," he said gruffly, raising his arm in the air, demanding silence. "We have a press release available for you all. Thank you for coming."

He ushered Alex out the door, as the journalists continued their barrage of questioning.

"Do you think it was a bomb?"

"Do you think anti-Castro groups were behind this?"

"Ms. Miletic …"

Fame entered Alex's anonymous life as Miami embraced its newest celebrity journalist. Good looking, young, a survivor—the perfect lead in to the evening news. Jose knew the local media would be milking this story for a few days.

"Let's go home, *mi amor*," whispered the aging editor as he checked Alex out of the hospital. "It's enough for today." He placed a fatherly arm around her shoulders as Alex rested her aching head on his burly chest.

Jose was a curmudgeon *extraordinaire*. Self-possessed and imperious, he came from a long line of passionate Cuban men. His caramel brown skin, tanned to perfection was framed by a neatly cropped ashen beard, belying his fifty plus years. Jose demanded perfection and was not above throwing tantrums like a five-year-old, but he groomed novice reporters into world class journalists. His commitment was 120 percent, and despite the fact that she sometimes infuriated him, his love for Alex was immeasurable.

The newsroom was his family. Since the death of his wife, Teresa, and his only child, Manuel, he worked sixteen-hour days returning to an empty home with take-out Chinese and a bottle of scotch.

Armed with a graduate degree in journalism from Columbia, an ancient copy of his Bible, Strunk & White's *Elements of Style* and a secret stash of Johnny Walker Black, Jose waged a war against crime, corruption and deception like a man possessed. Never again would he tolerate oppression. He longed for Cuba's soil and the abolition of Castro's tyranny. One day his people would be free, no longer drowning, within sight of liberty. One day he would go back to his birthplace and the vista of his human heart—Havana. Until then, he served as teacher, sage, and *padre* to his misbegotten crew.

As the voice of the community, the paper had a moral and ethical obligation to serve its bizarre medley of citizens. Jose's reporters were warriors, in ruthless pursuit of the truth and a pay check, and this was their proving ground.

"I feel like I dipped into madness," said Alex after a breath.

"Shhh, you need some rest," Jose told her, as if apologizing. "Jason's waiting downstairs and he's not pissed off, just worried. As much as you torture him."

Alex smiled and obliged reluctantly, her mind drifting as she walked down the hospital corridor alongside the only man she trusted. Then she saw them. Attorneys lined up like hyenas, sniffing negligence and settlement as they roamed the corridors.

"Ann, I want you to prepare a complaint. That paramedic I've been slipping C-notes to has finally earned his slush fund," shouted an obese man into his cell phone, an unlit cigarette dangling from his lips. "This one's as easy as a prom queen on roofies."

John Q. Esquire smelled money. He paced back and forth, smirking at the thought of what a jury might award a grandmother of five who had lost two fingers.

Alex's dark eyes narrowed. "Viper from hell," she snarled in revulsion. "Must have been comatose to hire a leech like him."

"*Tranquilo*. Not every battle is yours," comforted Jose as he ushered her out the front door.

The explosion was the biggest story in South Beach since the shootout at rap star Shakur's nightclub six months ago when an enraged patron having found his girlfriend flirting in the shadows with another famous rapper had opened fire on the crowded dance floor, killing two and injuring twenty. And, murder Miami-style meant big bucks. Nothing was sacred. Not since the days of the warring Colombian drug lords in the early 80s has the city seen such periodic bloodbaths. It's rebirth claimed lives—a sacrifice to the gods of prosperity.

Jose and Alex stepped out into the fading Miami sunlight. A gentle Atlantic breeze blew through an umbrella of palm trees, caressing her face, bringing with it a half-hearted promise of relief from the heat.

"I know what you're thinking, Jose," Alex said as she shielded her eyes. "But, this isn't just one of your bizarre run-of-the-mill stories. I just know it."

"Listen, *mi hija*. This town has as many strange stories as it has people," Jose told her in a flat voice. "When you've named as many streets after convicted malefactors as we have, nothing is sacred, not even a bunch of grannies getting blown up by a gas leak."

"But …"

"But nothing. Here's Jason. Go home. We'll talk tomorrow." Jose kissed her on the forehead as he escorted her towards Jason's Miata.

"V*aja con dios.*"

Alex slumped in the passenger seat as the car pulled away, leaving Jose standing at the curb.

"You had me real scared there for a minute, pumpkin," said Jason as he reached across the stick shift for her hand.

"I hate when you call me a vegetable," Alex retorted, pulling her hand away.

Jason smiled and continued in a tone between mockery and homage. "And to think I was worried. They'd need more than a few tons of flammable ·petroleum gas to make a dent in that hardass personality of yours."

"I'm sorry, Jason, but I'm really disturbed," she said, a tinge of strain in her voice.

"Well, we know that."

"No, I'm serious, you jackass. I saw a someone in the lobby right before the blast and I know in my gut he had something to do with it," continued Alex as she twirled an unlit cigarette.

"Maybe the gas company sent over a repair man and it blew as he was working on the leak," Jason suggested.

"Maybe I should talk with someone who actually has an IQ," she said, turning away to light the cigarette.

"You *are* feeling much better," stressed Jason as he turned onto Alex's block. "Seriously, honey, you need to lay off the booze and cigarettes for a while. Your cynical mind is starting to see conspiracy where there is none."

Alex pouted as Jason escorted her up the stairs to her second floor apartment.

An erotic tango flowed over the balcony from the building next door as laughter and the clinking of glasses accompanied the hypnotic beat. A bit early for a Tuesday evening, but then again, this was South Beach.

A tall, lanky figure stood in the shadows of the balcony a few feet away and Alex smelled the aroma of Turkish coffee bringing with it the sweet smell of home. Suddenly her mother appeared out of the shadows, holding a tiny Turkish coffee cup in her long, dainty hand. She was beautiful—tall, blond, green-eyed and youthful. Placing the cup on the balcony railing, she opened her arms to her daughter.

"Alexandra. *Macane*." The childhood nickname slipped joyously through her mother's lips. As a child, Alex had resembled a kitten toying with a ball of string, absorbed for a second, then bouncing off to the next distraction. Only her mother and Teta Maria called her by her birth name, Alexandra.

Alex's eyes softened. She was suddenly gentle, vulnerable and deliciously moppet-like as she jumped up and down in joy. Jason watched as she ran into her mother's open embrace and his heart melted.

After a dozen kisses, Alex left the matriarchal enfold and ran for the kitchen, a skip in her step.

"*Hvala bogu*," said her mother as she crossed herself. "The war has taken too many already."

Jason raised an eyebrow, perplexed by her comment.

"Thank you for calling me," whispered Zvona as she reached for his hand. "She's so stubborn at times."

"No one knows that better than I do," Jason replied, shaking his head. "You should talk with her. She's entertaining some crazy idea that the explosion was deliberately rigged by some phantom bomber. It's nuts! Who would bomb a geriatric facility?"

Zvona sighed. "Man may age," she declared meaningfully, "but his crimes don't whither with time."

"Jesus, Zvona, now I know where she gets her morbid disposition from."

"Don't use God's name in vain."

"I'm sorry but ..."

"Peace doesn't exist. There is only the momentary absence of war, Jason. Cease fires last a week, a month, maybe fifty years, but seething revenge eventually rears its ugly head," Zvona said as she took Jason's face between her delicate hands.

She looked deeply into the young man's hazel eyes. "You can't run away from your legacy," she told him in a low, heavyhearted voice. "Eyes that have

24

witnessed death are no longer innocent my child. Shallow graves are eventually uncovered. The souls of those who have been wronged won't rest in peace until justice has been served."

"What kind of justice are you talking about? We're not at war here. We're in South Beach."

"There's much you don't know or understand, Jason," Zvona explained, a weary sadness in her gaze. "We're at war in Yugoslavia. There's much at stake and the borders are ill-defined. It's not just about the Croats, Serbs and the Muslims. It's about all the international interests who stand to make a huge profit and who will do anything and everything to ensure that the war continues."

"This is all a bit over my head, Zvona. Remember, I'm a Sports Reporter, not Christiane Amanpour," Jason said as a rush of hot wind blew over the balcony.

Alex's mother smiled sadly, her eyes shining in the dim light. "It's everyone's responsibility to discover the truth."

Suddenly, someone cried "*Opah*" and a burst of folkloric music poured into the room. As Jason stood staring about him in amazement, a Rubenesque woman joined them from the kitchen to cradle Alex in her arms.

"It's my Teta Maria," Alex exclaimed as the two women began to dance to a soulful melody of mandolins, violins and accordions, blending rhythms from the Croatian countryside. Aunt and niece twirled across the room to the balcony where Zvona and Jason stood watching, and Teta Maria grabbed Jason's arm to join them.

"Not only am I an American, but I'm an American without rhythm!" Jason protested, shaking his head as Teta Maria led him to the middle of the room.

He tried to escape from the circle that the three gyrating women had formed, but gave up in the end. Jason laughed and finally joined in, clapping his hands and clumsily shuffling his feet.

They danced, they sang, they tried to forget.

Veceras mi dobri ljudi
Nemojte mista pricati
Neka suze mirno teku
Pa ce manje boljeti.

Tonight good people
Don't speak

Let tears gently flow
So we'll suffer less.

"Now we eat," Teta Maria exclaimed, clapping her hands and ushering all three into the air-conditioned kitchen for the feast, leaving the thick, buttery Miami heat behind.

The smell of stuffed green peppers, sour cabbage and baklava tantalized their taste buds as the music dimmed to a distant echo and Alex smiled an insouciant smile. She had come home.

CHAPTER FOUR
SONS OF THE BLACK HAND

"The Bible tells us to love our neighbors
And also love our enemies;
Probably because they are generally the same people."
Gilbert K. Chesterton

The invasion took place in the late 1980s and had taken South Beach by storm, infiltrating the once tranquil Art Deco neighborhood and transforming the fifteen-block sector into a nonstop sexual carnival. The invader was barely twenty, six foot tall and blond. The modeling industry had discovered the tropical colors and the inviting backdrops of this once sleepy, oceanside town. And, where models went, money and men weren't too far behind. Haute couture boutiques, chic restaurants, trendy nightclubs, salons, spas, makeup and con artists—every nook and cranny was occupied by someone looking to make a buck and get laid.

Misha fit right in. His thick, dark ponytail, its ends curly due to the humidity, was pulled severely off his face and accentuated his beautiful cheekbones and piercing, predatory, black eyes. His Levis framed his taut physique so tightly that the "boys" creamed as he walked by, a slight limp in his gait.

"Oje, mi corazon," yelped a diminutive Cuban member of the gay brigade. *"Te quiero!* "

Misha stared with arcane bemusement then flung a lighted cigarette in the young man's direction.

"Oh, he's so *cruel*," the gay man cried out seductively to his pleasure seeking entourage. Buffed and brazen, the young men were out for another night of sexual prowling on Ocean Drive.

Misha meandered through a sunburned crowd of German tourists starry-eyed and drunk after a meal of *arroz con pollo* and tequila, busy planning a trip to Disney World the next day.

He entered an alleyway between the News Café and a newly opened nightclub next door. At eleven, the discotheque was empty, music filling the void. Miami embraced the mambo and salsa, swinging to the erotic, vibrant beat. Celia Cruz's voice a sublime aphrodisiac—the muse and artist of *la musica latina* singing "Guantanamera." Misha headed behind the mahogany bar, adorned with stainless steel barstools as a burly man in his forties emerged from behind a burgundy curtain, staring ominously.

"*Zdravo*, Misha," Peja greeted him, clearly annoyed at the young man's tardiness. They hugged and Misha kissed his friend three times on alternating cheeks.

"I had to be sure I wasn't followed," he explained, his dark eyes alert and searching.

"What happened?" Peja said, looking down at Misha's leg. "What's with the limp? You said you'd be careful."

"Oh, nothing. My timing was off by a few seconds. I was distracted by a woman," answered Misha, a mile-wide smile lighting up his face.

"Vera will kill you and so will I. Keep focused, I can't afford to lose you to your dick," Peja said as he grabbed Misha behind the neck and dragged him to a dimly-lit, smoke filled room behind the curtain.

Six men sat at a round table, a bottle of slivovitz prominently placed next to a cigar box. They rose and greeted the prodigal son one at a time, hugging and kissing, a sense of nationalism flowing like a dark undercurrent.

Misha poured himself a shot glass of the clear plum brandy and tossed it down his throat. The others followed in unison, raising their hands to God.

"*Ziveli*!" To life!

"You have the name?" asked Misha.

Peja nodded.

"Good. Tomorrow's the day. Let's get started."

Misha sat at the table as another glass was poured. He reached for the cigar box. Hoyo de Monterrey Double Corona. Perfect. Thank you, Uncle Fidel.

All he needed was Semtex (a creamy yellow play-do explosive substance), a detonator, a triggering mechanism and tobacco leaves. He got to work meticulously placing the ingredients of destruction in neat sequence. The group of men hurriedly extinguished their cigarettes, fidgeting anxiously, stepping two feet from the table.

Misha lit another cigarette, inhaled deeply and smiled as they retreated.

"Barbarians. You only know how to use knives," he teased, shaking out the match.

Misha reached for the plastic substance with his large peasant hands. Placing the square block in front of him, he started to roll the deadly material into a miniature missile, four inches long and less than an inch thick.

When completed, the explosive charge resembled a cigar with two exposed wires. Misha inserted the detonator into the explosive material, reached for the tobacco leaves and like a Cuban cigar maker, he carefully wrapped the brownish leaves around the device. Sitting back, he examined his masterpiece. Fine enough to smoke.

Misha reached for the cigar box and placed the deadly cigar inside, waiting to connect the wires to the trigger mechanism, setting up the electrical circuit. The opening of the box would pull the metal wires, triggering the switch and *Auf Widersehen*!

Misha knew there were two classes of explosives. High-order and low-order explosives, the difference being the rate or velocity of burning. Low velocity explosives, such as black powder, were slow burning and often used in pipe-bombs and kindred improvised explosives while high-order devices required an explosive shock to initiate detonation. He chose the latter. The high-order explosives delivered the blast wave or "shock front" effect caused by the explosion and would become as visible as a rapidly moving white shell. Misha only had to add some wire fragments and small metal shards around the main charge for the devastating fragmentation result—the most deadly effect of the bomb. The young ammunitions expert smiled as he stroked the sides of the finely crafted oak case. His creation was simple, effective and immediate.

Opening the box, Misha stared at the artistic etching of a black hand grasping the blade of a knife.

"He'll look into the eyes of the beast before he dies!" he said, wiping away a tear. "He will know who and why, and then let God judge him to hell for all eternity."

The gang of men surrounded Misha and said in unison, "*Za sve pravoslvane dushe.*" For all the Orthodox souls, they repeated.

Peja poured Misha another glass of slivovitz and crossed himself in benediction.

"We'll have to work faster," he explained nervously, stroking his walrus-like mustache. "Another shipment is due out at the end of the month."

"It won't reach its destination," assured Misha as he continued to work on the detonating device. His collar was soaked with sweat, his cool demeanor betrayed by a ring of perspiration.

"Dubravka would have been proud," said Peja solemnly as he placed his hand on Misha's burly shoulder. "She's looking down on you now as a true defender of the people. *Ona je sa bogom.* Remember, she's with God now."

Misha placed the tools on the table and sat back. He felt his mother's guiding presence as strongly as he had when he was a young boy. Dubravka had always been a survivor. As a child during World War II, she had crawled in the chicken coop to hide from the armed gang of Croatian Ustashe when they came for Misha's Serbian grandfather. She had listened as they had beaten him and then led him away to Jasenovac, the worst concentration camp in Croatia. Later, she ran secret messages to the Partisans who hid in the surrounding hills, contributing to the war effort as a clandestine child spy.

Misha closed his eyes and remembered his mother's thick peasant thighs and her soothing smell of sweet sweat and flour mixed with the fresh scent of earth. Nothing could touch him then nor now. He was protected. She was always with him.

Misha drank another shot of slivovitz and he carefully closed the box.

"Boom! *Jebem ti*! Fuck you!"

"*Jebem ti*," shouted Misha's nationalistic gang as they downed the last of the plum brandy.

Peja finished his glass of slivovitz and turned to Misha, his eyes darting back and forth from him to the door. "It's time to leave," he said. "There's a line waiting to get in and with the overflow, I'm concerned."

"Let's celebrate the victory of our next battle," said Misha, raising his glass, fatigue pulling at his heavy eyelids.

Slamming the glass on the table, he headed for the back exit.

"Keep it in your pants!" yelled Peja behind him. Misha waived and continued walking into the night.

At three in the morning, the streets were full of revelry. Palm tree fronds swayed in the gentle breeze in harmony with drunken human gyrations. The squeals and groans of lusty play permeated the stifling ninety degree weather. Tanned bodies glistened in the street light.

Misha walked back to his two-story hotel on 6th street in the heart of South Beach. A pretty brunette sat in the lobby bar, welcoming him with her big, brown puppy dog eyes. As Misha walked up the stairs to his room, she followed, swaying to the beat of Tito Puente.

Misha turned on the ceiling fan, opening the jalousie windows for maximum breeze while she entered, securing the chain lock.

Her long fingers caressed her shoulders as she slipped her white, silk camisole down to her hips revealing crimson, erect nipples. Misha approached and cupped one of her breasts, playing with the nipple gently. A sweet moan escaped her lips.

"Not tonight, Vera," Misha said as he pulled away. "I need to sleep."

"But I've been waiting for you all night," she reminded him, a petulant edge to her voice. "I'm not going to wait for you forever like my mother waited for my father. I'm just not!"

Misha turned around and slapped her face with the back of his hand. "You'll wait for as long as you have to wait." He started to slowly undress.

"I'm not doing this anymore!" Vera cried as she sat on the side of the bed weeping. "I followed you. Believed in you. *Idi kod djavola*! To hell with you!"

Storming into the bathroom, she slammed the door and turned on the shower. He listened as she tossed toiletries about, cursing his name.

Misha looked at himself in the oval mirror on the wall across from his double bed, his eyes resting on a small, black indelible mark on his left pectoral. Stepping closer, he caressed the small tattoo of a black hand grasping the blade of a dagger.

"*Za tebe*." For you, he whispered. Raising his arms, he began to dance as he sang an old Serbian tune.

Tamo daleko
Daleko kraj mora
Tamo je selo moje
Tamo je ljubav moja

Far, far away
Across the sea
There is where my village lies
There is where my love lies

Misha closed his eyes as his baritone voice lowered to a whisper, his mouth mimicking the last few verses silently. He slipped under the white, cotton sheet as Vera continued her violent monologue. He needed his rest. Nothing else mattered.

Every night he dreamed of a wolf lurking in the forest, slowly following its prey, the pack closing in for the kill. Now, as he closed his eyes, he heard the wolf howl, beckoning Misha to join the nocturnal hunt.

CHAPTER FIVE
COMRADES IN ARMS

"The only thing new in this world is the history you don't know."
Harry Truman

The yelling could be heard all the way down the plushly carpeted, mahogany corridor and into the elevator. Portraits of dead board members hung on the walls, their images encased in gaudy faux gold frames. Corporate gentility's attempt at immortality. Bald, fat and long gone, the fathers carefully eyed the current going-ons in amusement. The secretaries, tall, blond and dressed in short, stylish yuppie skirts and summer blouses, ran to their cubicles and placed dictaphone headsets in their ears. Someone's head was about to roll and it wasn't going to be a pretty sight. Another poor young executive would quickly emerge from the big man's office, his tail between his legs, the blood drained from his face. Just a typical day at corporate headquarters of Brand Industries, the top gun and ammunitions conglomerate in America.

Wilhelm Heidrich, president and CEO, sat in his fine leather chair, a spreadsheet in one hand, a red pen in the other. Immaculately dressed in an Armani suit and black wing tipped oxfords, he sported a $15,000 presidential gold Rolex. A slight paunch protruded from behind the double-breasted jacket, but it was nothing that a week of skiing in Aspen wouldn't cure.

"Fuck the environmental reports and those 'Earth First' pansies," Wilhelm shouted. "We're not planting organic soya beans. We're manufacturing tools of modern warfare."

33

Crumpling the report into a tight ball, he tossed it at the pale Public Relations Vice President seated across from his large oak desk.

The young man chewed on his bleeding, raw cuticles as he bent over to pick up the mangled report. The dark circles under his large brown eyes betrayed his attempt to appear resilient, and his stomach churned. His legs twitched under the table, absorbing the tongue-lashing. He'd live through yet another meeting.

"Yes,sir," he said wearily, flipping through the hundreds of pages of a report sitting on his lap. "I understand, but I need to address these questions. The radioactive materials have apparently contaminated surface and ground water and the surrounding land. The environmental groups have found eighteen times the background level up to nine-tenths of a mile away and the town has the second highest level of thyroid cancer in the state. That's two-and-one-half times the state average."

"We don't have to address shit!" Wilhelm told him stiffly. "If the Department of Defense and Los Alamos are satisfied, then so am I."

"Yes,sir," answered the young man, placing the report into a folder. "I'll draft the usual press release."

"You're learning, son."

Wilhelm hired only the best. Nothing like stock options to turn young, bright grads into whipping boys.

"Now, get out," Wilhelm said gruffly as he turned to his computer and logged in.

His youthful executive sheepishly exited the room and ran to his office for a swig of Mylanta. Unfortunately, Wharton business school hadn't prepared him for either Wilhelm Heidrich or the "Silver Bullet" controversy.

The "Hatchet Man" ran his company like a sadistic drill sergeant in boot camp, demanding blood from his most loyal soldiers. But he was a financial miracle worker. Under his command, productivity had skyrocketed, propelling the stock price to new highs. The stockholders loved him. And as long as the stock soared, so did he.

Wilhelm Heidrich had barrelled his way into corporate stardom. As featured in the latest edition of *Fortune* magazine and *Guns & Ammo*, Wilhelm had introduced "Silver Bullets" or depleted uranium (DU) special bullets. These controversial rounds were used by US warplanes to destroy Iraqi tanks and armored vehicles during the Persian Gulf War. God bless the USA and the Second Amendment! The company had made a killing.

The depleted uranium bullets were the pride of the American arsenal and considered a super weapon of the 1990s. Defeating the toughest armored vehicles, they packed a knock-out punch from the solid depleted uranium metal rods in the shells. During the Gulf War, the United States had fired as many as one million depleted uranium rounds. At high speed, the bullets slice through tank armor like a hot knife through butter, triggering explosive content and creating a fire hot enough to melt aluminum. The men in the target vehicles had died in their metal coffins.

Wilhelm Heidrich was a star with the US military. The depleted uranium bullets were cheap to produce and their homicidal effectiveness made them one of the most prized weapons in the American military armory since they punctured tanks like beer cans.

Originally designed in the 1970s to destroy heavily armored Russian T-72 tanks, the depleted uranium bullets were made from low-level radioactive waste left over from the making of nuclear bombs and nuclear fuel. Known as radioactive isotope U-238, it had a half-life of 4.5 billion years. Oh well, Wilhelm figured he'd be dead by then anyway.

He stared at his computer screen's ticker tape, indicating that his company's stock was up two percent. War was such good business. And, a subsequent shipment totalling thousands of tons of small arms, mortars, anti-tank weapons and surface-to-air missiles was due to leave China in a couple of days, increasing his profit margin. Within two weeks, the boys in Bosnia would have enough to last them a while.

Even though the United Nations arms embargo was in effect, the United States Congress was pushing for unilateral lifting of the ban in order to help out the beleaguered Bosnian government forces battered by the better-armed Serb opponents. Wilhelm knew that it was only a matter of time before the embargo was lifted, and until then, the Bosnians would pay a hefty premium for the ammunition. Even the president of the United States tacitly approved his shipments, as long as the pipeline remained hidden from the public eye.

Public sentiment supported the Muslim-led government and opposed the Serb aggressors, but the Congress still couldn't publicly go along with the President and lift the ban. At least not yet. And, until then, Wilhelm was more than happy to supply the freedom fighters with all the arms and ammunition they needed. He had no quarrel with the Bosnian Muslims, the IRA, the guerillas in Colombia or any other group who was willing to pay his price. He had one allegiance and one allegiance only—to the almighty greenback.

The reality was that these international warring groups, politically motivated or not, all relied on the illegal or "black" market for guns, grenades, mortars, and other weapons that sustained their warfare, terrorism or criminal networks. Private dealers such as Wilhelm and his cronies had ties with various governments' intelligence agencies and they knowingly violated the arms sales laws or policies for commercial gain. It was a free market working within the laws of supply and demand.

Wilhelm sat reviewing his profit and loss statement when the phone rang. He glanced at his watch and realized that a reporter from the *New York Times* was due to call at any moment about a story on the Gulf War Syndrome. Apparently thousands of soldiers had come down with some serious ailments and were claiming that the use of depleted uranium bullets might have something to do with it.

"Mr. Heidrich, I have Mr. Freedman on the line from the *New York Times*," announced his secretary.

"Alright, put him through," replied Wilhelm, pressing the record button on his phone. He couldn't be too careful. Journalists were always misquoting him.

"Marty, great to hear from you. How's the family?" asked Wilhelm with feigned enthusiasm.

"Very good. How was your trip to Miami?" replied the journalist.

"I had a funeral to attend."

"Sorry to hear that. A family member?" asked the reporter.

"You could say that," Wilhelm responded, a tinge of regret in his voice. "Someone I've known for a long time."

"Well, I suppose we all need to go sometime," replied the newshound dismissively. "Listen, Wilhelm, I won't keep you long but I do need a quote for a piece I'm doing on the Gulf War Syndrome."

"Shoot."

"Very funny."

"No, seriously. How much scientific research did your company do to investigate the possible health effects on soldiers once the bullets blew up and the uranium was exposed to air?"

"You know, Marty," Wilhelm said, his voice as smooth as oil. "These are difficult times, especially after the Persian Gulf War and now with the war in Yugoslavia. We've worked very closely with the Department of Defense and Los Alamos National Laboratories to ensure that the weapons that our boys use are lethal on one end and on one end only—the enemy's. I've been speaking with our nation's representatives on a daily basis just to ensure that we as a country are prepared to deal with the threats in the world. War is serious business. Unfortunately, some are not prepared to psychologically deal with the fallout."

"Are you saying these soldiers who fought in the Persian Gulf War are imagining their symptoms?" the reporter asked him. "Are you saying it's psychosomatic?"

"All I'm saying is that there is no credible evidence to indicate that the depleted uranium bullets in any way are harmful to our military. These bullets are intended to provide a lethal force against our enemies and that's what they do," responded Wilhelm. "And we at Brand Industries are doing our part by supplying our men in uniform with whatever they need to fight the forces of evil."

"Okay, Wilhelm," the reporter said sharply, clearly annoyed by the public relations jargon. "But that doesn't answer my question. Apparently, there are thousands of our soldiers who are suffering from gastrointestinal, neurological, and muscular disorders. And since this is the first time that depleted uranium bullets have been used in battle, I think they're more than justified in exploring the possibility of a connection."

"I think we need to do everything we can as a nation to help our boys in uniform," the CEO responded, a bit aggressively, "I'm sure the Veteran's Administration will come through and provide them with all the help that they may need. Medical or otherwise."

"So, you are saying that it's psychosomatic?" the reporter pressed.

"I'm saying that there is no credible evidence to indicate that the use of the weaponry in the Persian Gulf has anything to do with their perceived illnesses," Wilhelm said, skillfully avoiding the question.

"Listen, Marty, sorry, but I have an important call coming through. Give my PR guy a call and we'll pick up where we left off. I appreciate your calling and trust me, I take this matter very seriously. Oh, and, Marty, always a pleasure talking with you," said Wilhelm as he hung up the phone and reached for the cedar cigar box on his desk.

"What a son of a bitch," he muttered to himself, a trace of humor in his voice. "I'll have to add him to the Christmas list."

The phone rang again as Wilhelm sat twirling an unlit cigar between the fingers of his right hand.

"Mr. Heidrich, I have Joseph Gruntler calling from Miami," said his secretary.

Wilhelm came to attention and pulled out the file sitting in his top drawer. "Put him through."

"Joseph, *mein Freund,* how are you?" inquired Wilhelm as he riffled through the papers.

"I thought you had things under control." said Joseph, on the verge of hysteria. "They got Hans!"

"I know they did," sighed Wilhelm as he opened a brown file on his desk marked "Private and Confidential" and flipped through the latest report with pictures of the bombings in San Diego, Michigan and Miami prominently displayed.

"Don't worry, Joseph," he said, his eyes worried. "I'm on top of things."

"Like hell you are! We've got a ticking time bomb—and you know I'm next! First, Fritz, then Eric, and now Hans …"

"Calm down," Wilhelm said as angry veins stood out on his forehead.

"I don't have to tell you that, if I go down, you'll be the next casualty," Joseph told him, hostility in his voice. His warning feigned authority, calling rank from times past.

"You know I will do everything to protect you," Wilhelm assured him, after a beat. "I owe my life to you. I will find them and they will be eliminated."

"I feel their presence. I know I'm next," replied Joseph, his voice cracking. "We're hunted animals. I knew one day …"

"Shut up!" William roared. "Joseph, *lassen sie das*." Stop that kind of talk. "No one can touch you," William continued as calmly as possible.

"Where are we with the Brotherhood?" Joseph persisted, sounding pitiful. "I'm not going down alone."

Wilhelm groaned, "You're never alone, Joseph. We're here for you. Just remember who you are. Everything is working out fine. The next shipment is due to leave in a couple of weeks and then we'll be home free."

"How did they find us after all these years?" Joseph demanded, his voice rising an octave.

"I don't know but I'm sure as hell going to find out," Wilhelm replied, closing his eyes momentarily. "Just sit tight, *mein Freund. Auf Weidersehen.*"

Wilhelm's crimson cheeks turned ghostly white as he hung up the phone. Reaching for the crime scene photographs on his desk, he tossed the pictures into the trash, lit a match and watched as the photographs crackled, sizzled and shrunk to tiny warped black cinders. But the images still vexed him.

The blood of his comrade Eric splattered on the walls. Hans' fake teeth the only remaining evidence of the old man's existence. Damn! This was not the work of an amateur. This guy was a pro. He needed to keep his composure. The best-laid plans are flawed and he would find his enemy. Every man has a weakness. Nothing mattered now except for the Brotherhood.

Wilhelm accepted his new mission with alacrity. The best defense is an offense, and his aegis was deadly.

Wilhelm rose and looked out the window of his thirtieth floor office. His palms were clammy and cold as he twisted the crimson-red ring on his pinky finger. Now only four such rings were worn by members of the Brotherhood, and he needed to insure the survival of the others.

Back at his desk, he reached for the phone and dialed. "Get here immediately," he ordered. "You're going to Miami."

This was war.

CHAPTER SIX
THE BEGINNING OF THE JOURNEY

"The only thing necessary for the triumph of evil is for good men to do nothing."
Edmund Burke

Headache. Tylenol. The desperate search. Alex riffled through her medicine cabinet seeking relief from the pounder threatening to spoil her good mood. A few too many shots of slivovitz and too little sleep. All this on the day she had survived a bombing, written the story of her life and seen her mystery man.

She and Jason had partied with her mother and Teta Maria until two in the morning, exchanging stories, nibbling on home baked bread, fine cheese and *"shunka,"* thinly sliced smoked pork, olives, cucumber and sour cream salad, stuffed cabbage leaves and, of course, the baklava. Teta Maria had apologized for the meagerness of the presentation, having only had a couple of hours to prepare the meal. Jason, overcome with culinary joy, had dived right in.

That morning he moaned beneath the covers, quivering occasionally in the freezing air-conditioned apartment. The jalousies were drawn against the sweltering heat outside and the morning shadows danced about the room as the drastic difference in temperature formed a layer of condensation on the windows.

"Wake up, sleepy head," Alex said affectionately, tapping Jason's protruding bottom.

"I think I'm half alive ... but mostly dead," responded Jason as he continued to moan.

"You need to have the right genetic predisposition to absorb our food and drink," Alex joked.

"That's putting it mildly," he noted drowsily.

"How about a cup of Turkish coffee?" Alex asked him, uncharacteristically solicitous. "You may as well stay in the spirit of the Balkans."

"You're so sweet this morning. Maybe we need to bomb you more often," murmured Jason as he rolled over and passed out.

Alex walked into the kitchen and put the beaten copper Turkish kettle on the stove. The aroma of the dark fine grains was enough to wake the dead. *This should do the trick,* she thought as she added a few heaping teaspoons of sugar and waited for the water to boil.

Alex sat on the counter and stared into space. Last night her mother had kissed every inch of her exposed skin from forehead to the tips of her fingers, as though she was forming a protective layer of love around her daughter. Coupled with Teta Maria's big *babushka* hugs, Alex had felt invincible. The two older women, overjoyed to have their baby alive and well, had fed her morsel by tasty morsel, catering to her every whim. She was spoiled rotten which was probably why the peaceful look on her face was seldom seen outside this matriarchal energy zone.

That morning, though, there was no peace. Alex leaned back against the white Formica cabinet, massaging her throbbing temples, and realizing all the kisses in the world wouldn't get rid of this ache. Damn, no pain killer. She slowly hopped across onto the cold kitchen tile floor and walked into the living room where she plopped down on the beige sectional couch and looked at the clock. Seven thirty. Still early. She had a moment to herself in the quiet of the morning.

Today was the beginning of the rest of my life, thought Alex.

Wrapping her burgundy silk robe about her like a blanket, she stared at the wedding picture of her parents. They looked so happy. Who would have known. Promises of lifelong devotion and passion turned like sour milk. Her parents fought. About politics, about religion, about whether there was enough oil on the salad. But her mother always said that one of the privileges of marriage was that you have someone to fight with.

Alex sighed as she thought about Jason nursing his hangover in the other room. He was a good man. For the last three years he has been by her side, trying to understand what made her tick. Why couldn't she just let him in? What was she afraid of? Not every relationship was doomed. Maybe "in love" just turned to love, familiarity and friendship. A genuine caring for each other. Who knows? Her parents never made it to that stage. Maybe it was impossible.

Alex's Catholic, Croatian grandmother hadn't even attended the wedding. Her daughter's marriage to an Orthodox Serb was too much for her to handle, and no amount of Hail Marys prevented the union. It was sacrilege. Her daughter had betrayed her church for passion.

Alex's grandmother died never uttering a word to her only son-in-law, cursing his name with her dying breath. He was no good. He would leave her. He was too much of a dreamer.

The family buried her in a small cemetery outside of Dubrovnik, not far from her birthplace, and Alex's father paid for the plot and the modest headstone out of his meager savings.

After three days of mourning, they had gone back to their lives. And, life was good for a little while. But that hadn't lasted.

Alex's eyes turned to another prominently placed photo on the mantle of the faux fireplace. A cherubic, naked baby sat joyfully cradled in her father's arms as he stood thigh deep in a pristine, blue sea, a few feet offshore. Their tanned bodies glistened in the Balkan sun as she reached curiously for the tiny waves. Alex could hear herself chuckle with joy. She had always loved the water. Frolicking in the waves or safe in her father's strong arms, Alex had never dreamt that anything could hurt her. They had felt protected by the city patron saint, St. Blaise, or Sveti Vlaho, as the locals called him.

Dubrovnik was mystical. A city born on the protruding rocks of the Adriatic, whipped and rivelled by the sea. George Bernard Shaw had been entranced by this beautiful seaside city and apparently Edward VIII's last trip abroad with his infamous Mrs. Simpson before they were married was to Dubrovnik and the Croatian Adriatic coast. Some of the locals had claimed that the ostracized couple even wanted to settle there after they were married.

Dubrovnik had been an independent, merchant republic for 700 years until it was abolished by Napoleon in 1806, carrying on trade with Turkey and India in the East as well as the Cape Verde Islands in Africa. The city had even had diplomatic relations with the English court in the middle ages, and its status was such that puissant and wealthy Venice was envious of this Croatian city on the other side of the Adriatic.

The old town, completed in the 13th century, remained virtually unchanged to the present day with its tall ramparts and two walled entrances to Stradun, the old city's promenade.

Alex's cottage-like home had been within the old city limits of Dubrovnik, enveloping her in history and lore. The moist cobblestone streets in the ancient city had formed a natural hopscotch playground for the children of the neighborhood. Old tales of queens, kings and battlefields fueled their imaginations as they played within the fortress walls. Across from the white sands which fronted the luxury hotels, lay the island of Lokrum. As legend would have it, King Richard the Lionheart had landed on the tiny island during a storm in 1190 and vowed to build a church on the very spot as a humble offer of thanks to God for saving his life.

Tales of nobility's extravagances and battles had filled Alex's childhood memory. As children, she and her friends had rowed to the island and explored the botanical gardens and ruins of a villa built by one of the Hapsburgs a few centuries ago.

In 1880, Archduke Rudolf v. Hapsburg, heir to the throne, had committed suicide on the island together with his mistress, the Baroness Vecera in Mayerling. They had decided that they had preferred to be together in death than separated in life, and locals believed the ill-fated couple's undying love could still be felt on the island. But rumors of the curse of Lokrum chased the children away by sunset when it was believed that ghosts of the past still roamed the ruins.

Alex's mother had worked in a small hotel by the beach, welcoming French and German tourists visiting in the summer months as she spoke both languages. During the winter she sewed beautiful, colorful garments and traditional hand woven tablecloths that she sold to tourists.

If only this simple life had been enough for her father. Never a card-carrying communist, he had smuggled Western goods into the port from Italy, hoping to turn a profit. The day his shipment of leather and fine textiles was confiscated, he was thrown into jail, not to be heard from again. He had forgotten or refused to grease someone in the communist fold's palm, and at the time, that was akin to major tax evasion or worse—treason. Everything was shared by the people unless you were in power. No one outside of the communist power elite profited without their knowledge. And no one profited without them getting their percentage. This was the rule. A rule that her father had arrogantly broken.

Ostracized by her fearful neighbors, Alex's distraught mother had struggled with the shame until finally she had arranged for a visitor's visa for herself and her eight-year-old daughter. They left for Paris never to return. At the age of ten, confused and displaced, Alex found herself on a boat to New York, leaving the City of Lights behind. Teta Maria who had lived in France and had worked in a *boulangerie* joined Alex and her mother on the journey to the United States. Alex closed her eyes and breathed in deeply. She could still smell the scent of fresh bread on her aunt's body to this day.

Now Alex wondered about her father. After all these years, was he still alive? What was he doing? Was he remarried? Did he have other children?

She quickly opened her eyes as she heard the boiling water spilling onto the heated electric grill in the kitchen. Alex jumped off the couch and ran, eager to taste her first cup of coffee.

Carefully measuring the finely ground coffee, Alex slowly added teaspoonful by teaspoonful until the water turned a rich black. She replaced the Turkish kettle on the burner and watched as bubbles percolated to the top and opened the kitchen cabinet to pull out the fragile, tiny cup and saucer. Alex breathed in the aroma as she poured. So much like the smell of home, a home from a long time ago.

"Here's to you, *tata*, wherever you are," Alex said softly, her lips barely moving, as she lifted the cup in the air. "*Ziveli*. To life."

CHAPTER SEVEN
A DAY OF RECKONING

"History is a vast early warning system."
Norman Cousins

The noose threatened to choke the very life out of him. God, he hated ties. His sweat-soaked collar rubbed against his irritated skin, leaving a crescent ring around his neck. The weather in Miami was brutal, but Joseph Gruntler never sacrificed dressing for the occasion. Donning a stylish suit, he entered the Memorial Classroom Building and walked up the three flights to his corner office.

Joseph walked down the long stark corridor, plastered with notices of summer employment opportunities and university organized trips to France and Italy to study languages, art and architecture. Silver spoon babies signed up by the dozens, their parents paying a hefty $5,000 tuition and board fee for eight weeks in Europe—a college student's version of camp which enabled them to escape the gruelling summer heat and stay out of their parents' hair. The trip was worth its weight in gold, even though it was a miracle if they retained an ounce of learning.

"*Buenos dias*, Dr. Gruntler," said Juanita, his cheery, plump, administrative assistant. She was waiting with a cup of Cuban coffee and a stack of mail and files.

"How are you on this beautiful day?" she asked, a tinge of sarcasm in her voice.

"Yes, yes, Mrs. Rodriguez," Joseph replied gruffly, wiping the sweat from his forehead. "This heat is unrelenting."

"Maybe you should loosen your tie," she suggested, smiling sympathetically at the suffering man. "That's why our men wear *guayaberas*. You need to let the skin breathe."

Joseph grunted something indecipherable in German and proceeded to his office and an elaborate stereo system. Bach's *Das alte Jahr Vergangen ist* soon filled the room as he shut the door behind him.

"I've printed out your schedule for the week and the Chancellor would like you to join him at a special luncheon honoring Commissioner Jackson," said Juanita as she walked through the door and placed his daily mail and files on the desk.

Joseph stared out the window at a group of freshman girls, dressed in halter tops and short shorts, awkwardly tossing a frisbee back to the jocks. Truants. *They should all be in class*, Joseph thought.

"There's a farewell party for Dr. Rivera this morning," Juanita told him. "We're all going. Would you like to come?"

"I think I've been to my fair share of farewell parties lately," Joseph said, his eyes misty and far away. He continued to stare out the window.

"Of course. I'm sorry. I forgot how close you and Professor Fritz were," Juanita said, her face turning a beet red. "Very well then. I'll be back in an hour."

Joseph looked at the pile on his desk, his eyes resting on a beautifully wrapped box. It was from the Chancellor's office, and it was about time. He smiled. The university must have met their fundraising goals with the most generous donation coming from Brand Industries.

But, with a $100 million general endowment fund, he deserved more than a year's supply of cigars. He mentally noted to speak with Wilhelm about that.

Joseph carefully unwrapped the box. Hojo de Monterrey Double Corona cigars. His favorite. At least the penny-pinching administrator had class and guts, thought Joseph, tearing off the wrapping paper with the eagerness of a child.

It was common knowledge that buying or possessing Cuban cigars in the United States was illegal. As part of the economic embargo against Cuba, the U.S. government considered Cuban-made cigars as contraband and most were confiscated if discovered by immigration officials.

What a stupid policy, thought Joseph. *Why deny the good people of this country one of the greatest pleasures on earth? Did the US government really think that Fidel Castro would succumb to economic pressure?* The black market ran everything anyway, and Cuban cigars were as popular as the Republican party on *Calle Ocho* near midtown Miami. The Cubans loved their coffee, their music, their cigars and Republican presidents. No self-respecting Cuban would be caught dead voting for a Democrat, not after what the exile community deemed to be the greatest betrayal by John F. Kennedy over the Bay of Pigs debacle and Jimmy Carter's attempt to normalize relations with the Cuban government. Besides, many Cubans believed Democrats too soft on communist credo, falling naturally into the Republican camp.

Joseph lovingly ran his fingers along the corners of the exquisite wooden box, reaching an almost sexual high. He inhaled deeply and detected a strange vanilla odor. Joseph frowned as he flipped up the bronze clasp and opened the box.

A bright blast momentarily blinded him, then proceeded to rip through the frail man's chest, neck and face, quickly sucking the very life out of his veins. His bloodcurdling scream was muffled by the shards of metal cutting through his vocal cords. He was horrified as he watched himself falling through a dark tunnel surrounded by the souls of Jasenovac who grasped at him and stared with their hollow eyes.

Joseph remembered counting to see how long it would take the Serbian prisoners to bleed to death as his soldiers cut their throats with specially designed butcher knives. He remembered his death squads killing the Jewish prisoners with axes, mallets and hammers, and then hanging them from trees and light poles. He remembered sipping his brandy as the gypsies burned alive in hot furnaces or boiled in cauldrons and turning a blind eye as small children drowned in the Sava River, several of them tied together at a time in a sack and thrown into the raging waters.

And as a testament to God, he finally remembered blessing the Catholic priests as they lead countless massacres, many armed, urging the fascist bands to kill the infidels with their crucifixes.

Then, he saw himself falling down a long tunnel towards a bright light. *Help me quickly, God, my soul is lost,* he prayed.

The last image was that of a black hand grasping the blade of a knife. And finally, he saw nothing but darkness as he vanished from life.

CHAPTER EIGHT
JUST ANOTHER DAY

"Once the toothpaste is out of the tube, it's hard to get it back in!"

H.R. Haldeman

The newsroom was abuzz like a colony of termites working on a wall. Jose stood nervously at the helm, yelling at the editorial assistant who fondled her belly button ring and clipped wire copy. His editors perused the morning papers and worked the phones, their keyboards hungry to slice at the news releases coming over the wire services. The tension mounted by the minute as the early edition had to be put to bed and Jose was way behind schedule.

Alex made her entrance at eight thirty, the earliest she had arrived in a year. Nothing like a front page story to get your blood flowing, she mused as she walked to her own little cubby hole at the east end of the large newsroom, overlooking Biscayne Bay. Her desk was littered with cards, a box of chocolates, a bottle of liquor and a few memos from the brass. She noticed that the publisher and editor-in-chief sent their perfunctory "Congratulations" and "Keep up the good work" corporate memos. Maybe she'd get a raise.

Alex sank down into her desk chair while the entire newsroom rose and clapped. The sports editor bowed at the waist and tossed a paper airplane which fluttered through the air and landed on her chair. "Great job, kid!" was the message on the wings. Alex blushed, mimicked a quick curtsy and then quickly sat back down, knowing she could expect nothing more than twenty seconds of fame from this jaded group as they went back to their terminals and their phones, looking for the next juicy story that would justify their existence.

Jose walked up behind her. "Don't think you can rest on past glories," he told her, offering her a styrofoam cup of steaming black Cuban coffee which was very little different from Turkish coffee, even down to the sugar content which was lethal in both.

"There's no pleasing you," remarked Alex as she took the cup gratefully.

"*Estas bien? Te ves cansada,*" he leaned down and whispered in her ear. Are you okay? You look tired.

"I'm fine, Jose," she said, smiling that million dollar smile that she knew always made him melt. "Actually, I'm more than fine."

He squeezed her shoulder, allowing his hand to rest there for a moment before retreating to his office to chew out the Arts and Entertainment reporter.

"*Mi madre*! Peter Mathiessen is arriving at the Book Fair on Thursday and I don't have your latest review," he announced. "It's unacceptable. You hear me?!"

"On my desk by five!" yelled Jose as he slammed his door shut.

The reporter, a newsroom veteran accustomed to her editor's mood swings, shrugged and continued with her interview. She winked at Alex. The old guy might carry on like a lunatic, but he had a heart of gold. Everyone in the newsroom knew he would go to bat for them. Two years ago when the parent company had been planning to streamline operations and lay off a few reporters, Jose had fought long and hard to keep them their jobs. Print journalism was a dying profession, and Jose the last of a moribund breed.

He was a purist from the old school. If you had the guts to get into this business and stay in it, he made sure you'd succeed. Everyone in the office agreed that he was the best. A leader in the newspaper guild, he was a bastion of tradition. Bring him a story he could sink his teeth into and he'd get you a raise. Bring him a story that made a difference in people's lives and he'd lay his job on the line. As far as Alex was concerned, they had broke the mold when they churned him out over fifty years ago.

A seasoned reporter with the tenacity of an enraged bull, he had dodged bullets in Vietnam, covering the war for the Associated Press. As a thirteen-year-old, Jose had been brought to the USA as part of the *Pedro Pan* airlift out of Cuba. Those children were special cargo. And, Jose was exceptional. He grew up with his *tia*, Isabel, in *el exilio*, his family denied exit. A few years back, he had almost died from sorrow when his wife and only son were killed in a car accident. The grief was so unbearable that he had turned to booze.

Lost in self-pity, he fished for a year in Key West and drank himself into oblivion, clinging to memories of better days.

And then he gave up the crutch of alcohol. No rhyme, no reason. He just stopped and called in a few favors. The publisher of *The Miami Gazette* had worked with Jose years ago when they had covered the war in Bangladesh in the early 1970s. Jose needed a reason to live again and the man at the helm of Miami's only English-language daily gave him one. Jose's drinking continued but only as a means to tolerate the pain. A functioning alcoholic, he obsessed about his work and lived for the daily stories he put to bed. As he often said, you're never alone when you have an obsession.

Jose was a man with a "big personality" and Alex liked that. She related to his idealism, his intelligence, his sorrow. They were like two peas in a miserable pod.

Downing the last of her coffee, she reached for the phone to check messages. A friend at the local ABC affiliate had called to congratulate her and asked for an exclusive interview. An hysterical woman clamored on for two minutes about the government poisoning her cat. And then there was Curtis Sommett, an agent with the Miami-based office of the Federal Bureau of Investigations. *Something was wrong,* thought Alex. The FBI never called journalists, and the strangest part was that she hadn't spoken with him since the big drug bust over a year ago when she needed a quote, and all she got out of him at that time was a "no comment."

Alex dialed the number anyway.

"Hi, this is Agent Sommett with the Federal Bureau of Investigations. Please leave your name, number and nature of your call and I will get back with you ASAP."

Beep.

"Alex Miletic with the *Miami Gazette* returning your call," she said, loud and clear. "I'm all ears. You know how to reach me. Later."

She hung up the phone just as Jose raced to her side. His face was etched by infectious anxiety.

"There's been a bombing," he told her hurriedly, the familiar wrinkles on his forehead deepened in worry.

"Where?" asked Alex, her stomach filling with panic.

"The University of Miami. A professor is dead."

"Jesus," muttered Alex under her breath. "When?"

"A few minutes ago at the Memorial Classroom building."

"Do we know who the victim is?" Alex asked, a sharp edge in her voice. Jose shrugged. "Some poli-sci professor named Joseph Gruntler."

"I'll get right over there," Alex said, grabbing her bag and tape recorder.

"You may be right, Alex," said Jose as he reached for Alex's hand, his voice lowered to a whisper. "This can't be coincidence. Three explosions in a week. *Ten quidado*. Be careful."

Alex turned toward him and nodded, her eyes on fire under the bright office lights. "Don't worry. I'll watch my back, but I must admit, it sure feels like I've stepped into a war zone," she told him as she started for the elevator. She was definitely on to something big.

CHAPTER NINE
THROW THE DOG A BONE

"It is hard to believe that a man is telling the truth when you know that you would lie if you were in his place."
H.L. Mencken

Alex arrived at the University of Miami campus and hurried to the site of the bombing. Yards of yellow tape surrounded the building, securing the area as a large crowd gathered, hoping to see a dead body.

"I'm sorry, ma'am, this area is off limits," said a tall, Coral Gables police officer as he stopped Alex from climbing the steps into the main entrance of the twenty-year-old building. A light bead of sweat glistened on his upper lip. "Watch your step. There's a lot of glass." He pointed to the shiny, razor sharp particles on the ground.

"I'm a reporter with the *Gazette*," Alex replied authoritatively, trying to muscle her way in by flashing her press pass.

The young cop stood his ground, gently placing a firm hand on Alex's shoulder. "I don't care if you're Mother Teresa. This is a crime scene. You can speak with our Information Officer. He's standing over there." The irritated peace officer pointed to a heavyset, Hispanic man surrounded by a television crew from the local CBS affiliate.

"You reporters, man ..." the police officer muttered under his breath, shaking his head with mock bemusement.

"Where would society be without us?" retorted Alex, smiling a devilish smirk.

"A hell of a lot better off ... I mean, no comment, ma'am," the rookie replied wryly as he continued eyeing the crowd.

"Shall I quote you?" taunted Alex without hesitation, turning to barrel through the onlookers. She looked around. There had to be a way in. Nothing was getting in the way of her story. She was on a roll.

Behind the garbage dumpster, she saw a door ajar. Alex slowly peeked through, seizing the opportunity. The door was open to the stairwell. She loved this part of her job. Slipping under the yellow police cordons, she entered the building.

Although no one was there, she heard voices echoing down the stairway. According to the police department, the bombing had taken place on the third floor. Alex's thin linen shirt clung to her back as she raced up the stairs, two at a time, her heart pounding as she reached the second landing. One more flight to go.

A door slammed shut and she recoiled against the wall. Panting, she prayed not to be discovered. Almost there. Just a few more steps.

Suddenly, she stopped. Someone was behind her. She felt the hot breath on her neck, his heavy hand on her shoulder, twisting her around to face him. Her heart raced then skipped a beat.

"What the hell are you doing here?" asked Curtis Sommett as he thrust her against the wall.

"Just doing my job," replied Alex as she sighed in relief, smiling half-heartedly.

"Don't give me that crap," the FBI agent said, sharply reprimanding her. "This is a secure crime scene."

"Maybe I couldn't wait for your call back. What are *you* doing here," asked Alex suspiciously, batting her eyes dramatically. She raised her eyebrows as she reached for her tape recorder.

"Look, girl, your ass is as good as gone," Sommett announced, as he grabbed her by the collar and forced her down two steps.

Alex stopped and sat down. "I'm not going anywhere until you talk to me," she said firmly.

"You obstinate bitch!" He sat down beside her. "What the hell do I have to do to get you out of here?"

"What happened here?" she asked as she flipped open her notepad.

"I'm not telling you anything!" he replied defiantly. His ebony skin glistened with sweat, but he was a cool as a cucumber. And, he was beautiful. Beautiful, strong, and unreadable. As one of the few black men in the bureau to rise through the ranks, it was clear to Alex that he wasn't going to risk anything to spoil his record.

"Look, you need to get out of here," ordered Sommett, shifting his regal body towards her.

"You owe me," replied Alex, reaching into her purse for a cigarette, rummaging a bit too long before she found the pack.

He grabbed the unlit cigarette and threw it down the stairwell. "Are you nuts?! You're going to get me fired! Besides, I owe you shit!"

"Why did you call me?" asked Alex tauntingly.

"A friendly check in is all."

"Like hell. Something is going on here and it's connected to the South Beach explosions," said Alex, with absolute aplomb. "Look, you know it and I know it. Don't give me the run around."

"No comment."

"That's what you gave me last year and I'm not settling for it. I'll start yelling …"

Sommett leaned over and clasped her mouth shut. Alex's eyes smiled. She knew he was just playing the bad cop routine and would give in because he wanted something from her. He slowly removed his hand.

"What do you need?" asked the agent acquiescing to her ardent demands.

"Take me up there."

"No fucking way!"

"I need to see the scene. You give me my scoop and I'll take care of you," Alex cajoled him.

"That's a joke if I ever heard one," he laughed. "You protecting me."

He leaned his six-foot three-inch frame against the wall and sighed. "God, you amuse me. Okay, I'll show you the scene. Stay behind me and keep that big mouth of yours shut."

Alex placed the palm of her hand over her mouth, her eyes widening with the gesture. "Speak no evil," she uttered, a lightness in her voice.

Sommett grabbed her under the arm and led her to the third floor.

Alex's shit-eating grin diminished as she shuffled behind her formidable source. Smoke, dirt and debris filled the hallway. He led her through the scene of destruction, sidestepping forensics experts and ATF agents gathering evidence. The door to the office swung on its bottom hinges as they entered Joseph Gruntler's tomb. The smell was horrendous. In Miami, nothing lasted long outside of refrigeration.

The body was still reclined in the leather chair. A thick pool of blood formed around the chair and desk, the edges already gelling in the heat.

Alex stared in horror. The corpse had no head or hands. Just a torso in tact, enveloped in its seething juices. She swallowed to keep the bile down. She put a kleenex to her mouth and nose and looked around.

Bits of skin, brain and skull bone clung to the wall directly behind the body, slowly sliding down, leaving streaks of blood much like a snail leaving a trail on dry ground.

This was obscene. Something out of a horror movie, but that wasn't pasta on the wall. Alex was frozen. She'd never seen a dead body before. Poor guy, they'd have to bury him in a closed casket.

"The way we figure it, it was a mail bomb of some kind," Sommett told her. "The main force of the blast took off his head and hands and then expanded outward, almost in a triangular shape, splattering the remains within a few feet's radius behind the victim. That's why his head and hands are gone and the rest of him looks pretty much intact."

"Who would do something like this?" asked Alex, almost to tears.

"Someone with a grudge, someone with a cause, someone who's got a screw loose. You name it," answered Sommett as he guided Alex around the body.

"You see, very little was damaged in front of the desk except for the windows. They shattered, but the music was still playing when we got here," added Sommett as he pointed as the elaborate stereo system.

"What was he listening to?" asked Alex, her eyes glued on the headless body.

"Some classical shit." The agent nonchalantly dismissed the dead man's final moments, flipping the tape cassettes on the floor with his shoe.

"This explosion was meant to kill him. No one else was hurt. There's some damage in the hallway, but nothing major. He got the brunt of it," said Sommett as he waived a junior investigator from the scene.

Alex turned a chalky white. The smell was getting to her. Unlike anything she ever smelled before. Some kind of chemical reaction … when your insides meet oxygen or something like that. She thought back to her chemistry class … she drew a blank. The room began to spin.

Turning, she headed out the door, weaving as she clumsily jumped over the files and books in her path, until she reached the corridor where she stood hyperventilating.

"I think you've seen enough," said Sommett, grabbing her by the elbow.

Alex fought that all too familiar feeling of wanting to heave. *Get a grip*, she told herself. *You're a professional. Death is ugly. It's finite.*

Then she turned and threw up. The other investigators in the hallway stared at her, clearly perplexed.

"First timer," Sommett said unsympathetically.

They went back to their work. Cold, rational, unemotional. It was their job. And, today, it was Alex's job too.

"That's great. I'll let forensics know it's not evidence," Sommett joked. "Welcome to reality, *baby girl*. You asked for it. That tough ass exterior only takes you so far."

It was, she thought, as though he was holding a mirror to her face, exposing her to herself. Maybe she *was* in over her head.

"You'd better stick to covering your clean little world," Sommett said, smugly.

"You know nothing about my world," she told him, an almost hysterical edge in her voice. "You think you're so cool, standing there smirking at me. You know I have you by the balls at this moment. You're surrounded by your cronies. And, I'm not budging until you give me something I can run with," Alex added, her eyes glaring and intense.

Tenacious and misdirected. She was in for trouble.

"I'm warning you …" he threatened her.

"And, I'm telling you I'm not going anywhere," responded Alex sharply.

Sommett hit the wall behind her head with his open palm. "You're as annoying as a yapping dog."

"Then throw this dog a bone," said Alex, color returning to her face.

"Okay, okay. You get your tight little ass out of here and look into Bloodstone," said Sommett, challenging Alex.

"Bloodstone?" asked Alex as she wrote the word in her flip pad, scribbling up a storm. "What, now I need to track down a gemologist to investigate some ancient stone? You can't just give a piece of the rock! I'm not going off on some wild goose chase!"

Sommett rolled his eyes and leaned within an inch of her face. "Shut up and listen. 1945. End of the war. Nazis. Do you think they were all strung up at Nuremberg?"

"What the hell are you implying?"

"You think I'm going to spoonfeed you? Go do your job. And don't call me. I'm done with small timers." He abruptly turned and walked down the hall, leaving Alex leaning against the wall with her head spinning and a lead.

Damn, she couldn't screw up again. The tide had changed. She had to make something of herself. No more unrealized dreams. No more "what ifs." She wasn't small fry.

Alex slowly walked slowly down the stairwell and out into the glaring sunshine, reaching inside her bag for her sunglasses. She still felt sick. Focused on the crowd, she wondered if anyone there had cared about the dead man? For that matter, did she?

Closing her eyes, Alex cupped her head in her hands as she leaned against the side of the building. The headless corpse danced in her mind, a supplicant of justice, his handless arms outstretched. What had the pathetic old man done to deserve this gruesome death?

The victim had his secrets, his enemies, his foibles, his dreams and, in the end, the loss of his dignity. Man was so proud, such a poorly misguided and miserable creature in this universe, egotistical enough to think that the world revolved solely around him.

No one had a monopoly on suffering.

Alex's mind raced in a million directions. Data overload!

She looked down at her shirt, flapping in the warm wind. A delicate fabric such as silk layered in sixteen folds could prevent a bullet from penetrating the natural flak jacket. One voice against oppression could change a nation's course. Maybe she could make a difference. Then again, maybe she was deluding herself.

Suddenly she felt exposed, vulnerable. Something had penetrated her protective layer, like a 22-caliber bullet tearing through flesh and bone. She instinctively wrapped her arms around her chest. Her heart pounded.

She was certain she was being watched.

CHAPTER TEN
BLOODSTONE

"Wars have never hurt anybody except the people who die."

Salvador Dali

Wilhelm Heidrich was a model of the Prussian officer. The elderly soldier missed his old days of service when his Bavarian orderly shined his black boots and maintained his Colonel's uniform in immaculate condition. Not a crease, not a smudge, nothing tainted the imperious warrior's presentation to the world. As it had been then, so it was now.

Wilhelm ran his fingers through a thick mound of glistening, silver hair and straightened his Hermes tie. The Colonel uniform long since replaced by a Hugo Boss suit, he grabbed the brush on the marble counter of the lush, private bathroom and vigorously stroked at the few pieces of lint. This was going to be a big meeting. He reached for the ornate, Louis XIV jewelry box and removed a red stone ring. Carefully placing it on the pinky of his right hand, he stared at the delicate engraving of a mighty eagle, its claws clenching the Iron Cross. What a work of art, a tribute to the sanctity of the Brotherhood. Now only three such rings existed on the hands of the living.

Wilhelm left his executive suite and gently cupped his right hand in his left to hide the ring from the few late night stragglers still milling about the office floor. He entered the elevator and reached for a keypad on the console, punching in the code—0427. Hitler's birthday. No one else in the building had access to the secret level of the company's headquarters.

The door closed as the lights dimmed and a computer voice automatically demanded in a slow and deliberate fashion, "Names and number of occupants."

"Heidrich, Wilhelm. *Eins*." The deadening silence reverberated in his ears as the computer ran voice recognition files.

A few seconds passed before the computer voice responded. "One. Wilhelm Heidrich. SS Number 43, 223." The door closed and the panel flashed: DESCENDING, LEVEL A-D.

Heidrich walked from the elevator into a long concrete corridor leading to a door that had been left ajar, awaiting his arrival. His shining, black shoes with steel reinforced heels, clicked in perfect rhythm to the march as he approached the room, holding his head high, his posture perfect. Deep in thought, Wilhelm twisted the ring over and over. Much was at stake.

The German marching song blared from behind the door. Wilhelm stood still as he listened to the music that transported his soul.

Alte Kameradan auf dem Marsch
Durchs Land schlieben Freundschaft felsenfest und treu.

Born in the German city of Halle near Lipzig, Wilhelm had been raised, along with his two brothers, Dieter and Hermann, in a cultured and musical family. Their mother, a Wagnerian opera singer, had died at the age of thirty-five of a protracted illness. After her death, Werner, their father, demanded perfection from his talented boys, believing in harsh discipline and frequent belt lashings. All three boys had excelled at athletics, including fencing and swimming. But rumors of Jewish blood haunted them. They needed to prove themselves.

In 1933, the Nazis celebrated Hitler's appointment as Chancellor of Germany. By 1935, the brothers had joined the *HJ-Streifendienst*, a recruitment camp for the SS or the *Schutzstaffel*.

Wernher had the face of an ascetic with intense eyes and an imposing presence. As a devoted Catholic, he demanded the boys attend church every Sunday and his tolerance for disobedience was non-existent, dishing out harsh punishment for the slightest childish infraction. Wilhelm never forgot that one Sunday in 1936 when Dieter, his youngest brother, was found wearing his *Hitler Jugend* uniform beneath the altar boy robe although Wilhelm had warned him against it. During the service, one of the boy's medals had fallen to the church floor, momentarily interrupting the priest's benediction.

Upon returning home, their father motioned for the three brothers to enter the barn just before lunch. His eyes were ice cold as he reached for his prized hiking stick. Dieter had barely survived the beating which had left him with a limp to this day, his tibia shattered into pieces by their father's consistent and well-placed blows. The brothers had watched only to be ordered subsequently to the lunch table as Dieter lay groaning in the barn, while their father slowly feasted on *weinerschnitzel* and potatoes, pouring himself glass after glass of wine. Not a word was spoken.

Three years later Wilhelm had turned in their father for criticizing Hitler's policies. Wernher was sent to Dachau under *Schuzhaft*, protective custody, for calling Hitler a "crazed Nazi maniac," and the boys rejoiced, believing themselves free of the devil once and for all.

The Heidrich boys had found a new family. A family that instilled pride and a sense of superiority in them and encouraged them to join the Hitler Youth, an organization to which, by 1939, eighty-two percent of youths within the Reich belonged.

They sang the Hitler Youth anthem, the *Fahnenlied* or Banner Song and passed both the physical test by running sixty meters in twelve seconds and tested their courage by jumping from a second story ledge into a canvass sack held by other HJ youths. They were willing to die for the cause. The Heidrich brothers were part of the elite, trained in the *Ordensburgen*, groomed for high level positions in the Nazi Party and for the greatest calling. The Brotherhood was alive and well and the world was theirs to conquer.

Rejoicing over their triumphs, the three brothers joined the SS and rose through the ranks. Indifferent to pain, without weakness or tenderness, they were efficient and loyal devotees of the Third Reich until the end.

Cherishing their valor, they chose not to forget, honoring the Brotherhood with monthly meetings. Wilhelm's fortune allowed them to have a secret hideaway, built two stories below ground level in the midst of Greenwich, Connecticut. The room had been decorated with stolen art, smuggled out of Germany after the fall of the Third Reich.

This was their sanctuary.

Ob in Not oder in Gefahr, stets zusammen
halten sie aufs neu'.

Now Wilhelm entered a room decorated with fine Oriental rugs and antique furniture. The oak panelled walls showcased their prized possessions, a few priceless masters interspersed with SS regalia. The temperature was cool, fresh air being piped in by small vents on the ceiling. The Colonel's icy blue eyes were withdrawn as he contemplated his last great battle.

Three old men, neatly dressed in dark suits, sat at a long mahogany table in the middle of the room, drinking brandy. They turned to face Wilhelm and slowly rose in unison extending their right arms. "*Heil Hitler, Herr Kolonel,*" they saluted him, and one, a burly, balding man handed him a glass of the liquor.

The Colonel remained silent. His hands cupped around the sifter, he paced before photographs of young men in uniform, vital, proud, unyielding. When the music faded into silence, he motioned for his brothers to retake their seats. His back stiff, Hermann stared straight ahead while Dieter shifted in his chair, one thumb polishing the brass handle of his black cane. The drumming of the Colonel's steel heels echoed—click, click, click—as he walked to the head of the table and placed the brandy snifter down.

Wilhelm placed his hand on Hermann's shoulder and then continued his slow march to an empty chair and caressed the finely carved back, running his fingers through the wooden waves of exquisite craftsmanship. His leather shoes creaked as he moved back towards Dieter.

"Wilhelm … *Herr Kolonel*, what is happening?" Dieter demanded in a quavering voice, his right hand shaking so that his ring rattled against the brass handle of his cane.

"Silence. I'm thinking," Heidrich told him gruffly. He leaned on the table, drumming a slow and methodical beat with his fingers.

"Someone's on to us," Hermann declared, leaning forward, his jaw muscles tightly clenched. He pointed at the three empty chairs before each of which a small candle flickered. "First Eric, then Fritz and Hans, and now our beloved Joseph."

"They're dead now," Heidrich said briskly, his eyes intently focused on the empty chairs. "I need to focus on the living."

"Joseph warned you. He told you he was next. You did nothing …" Dieter cried, rising to wave his cane in the air like a weapon.

Wilhelm glared at his youngest brother. "Sit down, Dieter," he told him, clenching his jaw muscles. "You've said enough."

"Are you going to protect us the way you protected me from our father?" Dieter's frail leg shook as he lowered his cane and collapsed in the chair.

"You were always weak and foolish," Wilhelm said, staring at him with cavernous, piercing eyes. "I'm warning you. I have always taken care of you. Now, stay silent."

"*Mein Kolonel*," interrupted Hermann, a bit aggressively. "What is this about?"

Wilhelm removed the holy ring, holding it before them. "It's about this."

"What do you mean? Do you think the Israelis, the *Mossad* is behind this?" asked Hermann, unfazed.

Wilhelm shook his head. "No. It's not their style. The Jews want public retribution, public closure. They prefer to abduct and bring to trial as they did with Eichmann."

"But we were just following orders!" Dieter said loudly, gulping his brandy, clinging to the sifter with trembling fingers. "We didn't kill anyone. We were only doing our duty."

The air was heavy with the pungent scent of fear. A few hours had been enough to overcome the initial shock of Joseph's death, but not the fear, fear that promised to cauterise what remained of Dieter's wounded soul.

"Shut up!" Wilhelm told them angrily, a blue vein pulsing on his left temple. "You were always a fool, Dieter. A man with such talents but no guts. No wonder you monitored head counts, *mein bruder*."

Hermann's eyes narrowed as his jaw clenched and unclenched. "Cowards. Afraid to show themselves. What kind of men are these?"

The robust, burly Major rose and slammed his fist on the table. "We will never succumb to this terrorism!"

"My, my Hermann. You still have the fire in you," taunted Wilhelm, a wry smile appearing on his stoic face. "That's why I put you in charge of training the Ustashe, our compatriots in Croatia. You had guts."

"But who are these men who are killing us one by one?" asked Dieter, confused and visibly shaking from the anxiety raking his feeble frame.

"A warrior people," explained Wilhelm, pursing his lips. "They're different from us. We come from a military nation."

Hermann's eyes blinked rapidly as he fumed. "After all these years? Almost everyone is dead. If it's not the Israelis then …"

"We all planned and sanctioned the killings," Wilhelm reminded him, shrugging distractedly, as if he were thinking of something more important than the systematic assassinations.

"But it was war, and it was such a long time ago," said Dieter dejectedly.

"The hunter sometimes become the hunted," Wilhelm told him. "We're the hunted now."

Hermann shook his head. "So, it's about Jasenovac."

Wilhelm nodded.

The concentration camp had been built on the "Road of Death" along the Sava River, chosen for its ideal location since the Zagreb-Belgrade railway, close to Jasenovac, was perfect for the transport of prisoners and the camp surrounded by the rivers Sava, Una and Velika Struga in the middle of swampy Lonjsko polje made escape impossible. Factories in nearby towns provided an ideal front to present the site as a work camp to the public. Entrusted to Department III of the Croatian Security Police, Jasenovac was the largest graveyard in the Balkans.[1]

In the winter of 1945, Wilhelm's troops dumped 123 freshly executed Partisan fighters into the semi-frozen Sava River, the bodies lost until springtime when the intact carcasses resurfaced from beneath the ice, turning the waterway into a river of blood. The bodies floated by the Croatian villages towards Belgrade as a gruesome reminder that resistance would be met with death. For every German wounded, fifty Serbs were killed. For every German soldier killed, 100 Serbs met their maker. With the war coming to an end, the krauts left their mark with a vengeance.

A few months after the mass execution, the death camp of five major and three smaller camps spreading out over 150 square miles were destroyed and burned, including most of the prisoners inside including women and children. It was the end of "the dark secret of the Holocaust."

During the war, the puppet Nazi state of Croatia had conceived a systematic policy of racial extermination dedicated to a clerical-fascist ideology influenced by both Nazism and extreme Roman Catholic fanaticism.[2]

As the German Transport Officer for Work Forces in the Third Reich, Wilhelm had helped to set up the camp in 1941. A year later he wrote in his personal diary, "Jasenovac is the most horrible of camps which can only be compared to Dante's Inferno."

Between 1941-1945, hundreds of thousands of Serbs, Jews, gypsies and other anti-fascists were murdered at this death camp.[3] During his quarterly camp inspections, Wilhelm, along with Marcone, the Pope's apostolic delegate who once strolled with him through the compound, were described by fellow German officers as "amateurs who appeared to sleepwalk through the entire bloodthirsty era." The truth was they didn't give a damn.

As talented numbers crunchers and soldiers, Wilhelm and the others helped turn the Nazi war machine into a money-making bonanza, making a fortune off the road of death along the Sava River.

Rage consumed Hermann as he reflected on the past. "I remember the faces as they stared at the execution squad," he told his brother. "These men were prepared to meet death. They gave up nothing to us, even during the interrogation."

Death had produced no triumph, no defeat, only a cleansing of what once existed. And, their deaths created a mythology inherited by the sons of suffering.

These men had finally recognized their assassin.

"Jesus. What about the shipment to Bosnia?" Hermann asked, apparently ready to pommel anything threatening his pocket book.

"We're still on course. So far, nothing has surfaced that might postpone the shipment. Our Chinese partners are assembling the weapons and are readying the cargo to depart Shanghai in a few days," responded Wilhelm coldly, delivering the status report as if he were presiding at a monthly corporate meeting.

"You can't be serious!" Dieter said. "How can you talk about business when they're planning on slaughtering us?" He sank back shivering into the plush chair as if the very life were about to be sucked out of him.

Hermann ignored his younger brother's emotional melt down as he poured himself another glass of brandy. "So, what are we going to do now?" he demanded.

"You're going to do nothing. It's really me they're after," said Wilhelm firmly. "I have already dispatched Aegis to Miami. The enemy will be eliminated."

Wilhelm pressed the play button on the remote control and lifted his glass in toast as the German hymn resonated in the room. "To our last victory."

CHAPTER ELEVEN
REMEMBERING

"It is a man's own mind, not his enemy or foe, that lures him to evil ways."
Buddha

Alex stared at the clock mounted on the white wall across from her desk as she clicked the "SEND" button on her computer screen. Her mind was racing, a result of genetic predisposition and adrenaline overdrive. What a day! She had just finished putting another front page story to bed, the second in three days, breaking a personal record. It was nine at night and her stomach growled like a beast about to devour her insides. She had worked non-stop all day, putting the University of Miami bombing story to bed. Ten cups of coffee, a pack of cigarettes and the recurring image of the headless corpse had curbed her appetite. Now, however, she felt like she could eat a horse.

The newsroom was empty except for the late night editor and the graveyard crew who were sitting playing computer solitaire, sharing a bucket of Kentucky Fried Chicken and listening to the police scanner. Much like cops, any idealism this jaded group had once possessed had long since been covered by a thick skin. What a bizarre lot journalists were, driven by the desire to unravel the human psyche, yet contemptuous of man's weaknesses.

Alex was coming to realize that she was just one of them, a vulturous creature circling, ready to pounce and to devour the facts and fiction of a story. But, like history, the article was written through the eyes of those extracting and interpreting events. Objectivity went against human nature. Alex could only do her best and hope that the story captured an essence of truth in the complicated web of many truths. She could only report through one set of eyes—her own.

Throwing her head back, she began a slow neck roll, hoping to dislodge some of the lactic acid buildup in her tired muscles. Alex always tended to philosophize when her blood sugar level dropped.

Her stomach roared again and she decided it was time to call it a day. There was nothing like Cuban food to soothe this savage, ravenous beast. She reached for the phone and dialed Jason's number.

"Hey, it's me," Alex cooed.

"Hi, babe. Hold on a second." In the background, Alex could hear the Miami Heat announcer's voice rising in jubilation.

"Jesus! What a shot! Glenn Rice is amazing," Jason yelled. "Sorry, honey. This game is unbelievable. What's new with you? Are you done yet?"

"Yes, I'm just about to leave and I'm starving. How about meeting me for some Cuban food?"

"I'd love to honey, but I'm watching this game. The team is playing in Atlanta and New York this week and this Chicago game is setting up my coverage for the week," Jason told her. "How about coming over after the game?"

Alex sighed as she had a million times before. There was no competing with the boob tube. She had lost her man to television for yet another night.

"I'll tell you what," Alex snapped. "When you grow up, you call me!"

Slamming the phone down, she grabbed her bag and headed out the door.

The elevator doors closed just as she heard her phone ring. Huffing, she pressed the button for the lobby.

What was it about men, sports and television. Alex was convinced they were born with a third chromosome, some primordial wiring that necessitated them to head to the couch the minute they walked through the door, grunting an indecipherable greeting, and grabbing for the remote control. Tossing their shoes in a corner and loosening their ties, they would proceed to yell at a square screen where grown men ran after a ball. During endless commercial breaks they would run to the refrigerator, grabbing another bottle of beer and a bag of Doritos off the counter, rushing back before the end of the commercial break about indigestion relief, totally addicted to cathode rays.

There had to be more to life than this, Alex thought. *God damn him.* What the hell was she doing? Here she was, a hot chick, and he wanted to spend the night masturbating over ten guys running across a court!

"What is up with you?" she muttered as she reached the parking lot. "Aaaah … get over yourself!"

She dropped the keys, and bending to retrieve them, noticed a pair of brown, sensible shoes staring her straight in the face. Alex slowly raised her head and smiled up at Jose who was looking down at her, rubbing at his gray beard as he always did when he was amused or concerned.

"Jason working again?" Jose asked.

"You call that work?

"*Mi amor*, he's a sports writer. What do you expect?" Wrapping his burly arm around her shoulders, he escorted Alex to her car as it began to drizzle.

Alex quickly started putting the top up on her convertible and they both jumped in as the rain came down in buckets, pummelling the roof and windshield with a vengeance.

"Listen to me," Jose said, cupping her face in his hands. "You know he's not right for you and still you hang on. He is who he is. Jason is a good man. A bit limited in his scope of the world, but he loves you. I've told you this so many times before but you continue to expect something he can't give you."

He released her and leaned back in his seat. "You know I love you like my own child, Alex. I don't know why. You're the most frustrating person I know, but I love you. Either accept him or move on."

Alex reached for a cigarette in her purse. "There are parts of him I love and parts of him I hate," she said fiercely. "It's so confusing. I don't like straddling the fence any more than he does, but I'm not ready to commit 100 percent. I feel like there's something missing."

Jose started rubbing her shoulder loosening the tight knot at the base of her neck.

"Then he's not the right one. Love is not something you try to create. It is or it isn't. *Amor*. It's *ingravida en el aire de tu beso*, in the tenous air of your kiss. *Tu sabe*."

"You still miss Teresa, don't you?" asked Alex as she reached for his hand, gently wrapping it in hers.

"Not a day goes by that I ask why I'm still alive and she died," Jose said sighing. "She was my life. *Que no cambiara ahor por la vida*. What I wouldn't give now for life." Tears came to his eyes. "Time doesn't take away the pain. In some cruel way, love is a beautiful prisoner."

They both stared at the city lights shimmering through the rivulets of rain. Jose sighed as he reached into his pocket and pulled out a handkerchief.

Alex turned to face him, admiring his strong, prominent profile. Such a lovely man. Full of passion and life, a weight of immeasurable sorrow drowning his fire. They were silent together, clinging to some common frame of silence and pain.

A streak of lightening abruptly brightened the dark sky. A loud crack of thunder followed, shaking both Jose and Alex from their silent musings. Alex gripped the steering wheel.

"You've had a hard day, Alexandra," Jose said in a low voice. "Go get something to eat."

"Do you want to come?"

"Not tonight, *mi hija*." Jose's sad, sunken eyes said it all. "You're doing good work you know. I'm very proud of you," said Jose, brushing a loose strand of her silky brunette hair from her face before leaning over and kissing her cheek. The bristles of his neatly cropped beard reminded her of her father's joyous embraces.

"*Buenas nochas*." Jose opened the car door and slipped into the stormy night.

She watched as he slowly walked toward Biscayne Boulevard, his shoulders slouched, impervious to the downpour, a gray ghost, drifting away, his image eerily enveloped by the falling rain. The raindrops fell like tears from the sky, crying for all lonely, suffering souls, desperately clinging to memories of lost love. Tonight, the heavens cried for Jose.

Alex turned on her windshield wipers and started the car. She noticed one other car in the employee parking lot turn on its headlights as she turned, heading east towards the Venetian Causeway.

Upon arriving on the barrier island that is Miami Beach, she headed to Ocean Drive. The normally crowded street was deserted except for a few homeless men lingering in storefront doorways, clinging to plastic wrappings. The neon signs blared "OPEN," hoping to entice the few potential customers committed to braving the weather. Parking was plentiful and Alex pulled into a metered spot near Lario's on the Beach, a quaint Cuban restaurant the locals embraced for its *Nuevo Latino* culture and visitors frequented hoping to get a glimpse of its famous owner, Gloria Estefan.

Alex threw her trusted, yellow rain jacket over her head and ran inside. She loved this charming and romantic Cuban restaurant. The service was wonderful, the food exquisite.

"*Buenas nochas, señorita*," said a smiling cherubic man, neatly dressed in a coat and tie, his white teeth gleaming against his weathered tan face. "Table for two?"

"No, *solamente para mi*," Alex replied, shrugging off her rain jacket.

"*Si señorita*. Please follow me. I bring you the wine list?" asked the maitre d' as he pulled out a chair at a small table by the window facing the quiet South Beach street. He quickly brushed off the seat with a white napkin.

"No. Actually, why don't you pick out a Chardonnay and bring me the bottle," said Alex, resigned to another night of solo drinking.

"Of course. I have a beautiful little bottle. A Chilean wine, very dry." He bowed slightly and headed behind the bar.

Alex sat watching the rain roll down the window behind the fine white curtains. She was alone except for a romantic couple groping each other at the opposite end of the long, narrow restaurant.

The maitre d' uncorked the bottle and poured a sip of wine into her glass, anticipating the obligatory swishing and tasting. Alex just stared at the glass. "Please *señor*, just pour the wine. I'm sure it's a fine vintage." Alex drank one glass before ordering and went on to quickly down a second.

Jose was right, thought Alex. She either needed to accept Jason or move on. This in between stuff was driving her nuts.

Alex sighed then settled comfortably in her seat. She may have been confused about men, but at least she knew what she wanted from the menu. *Ropa Vieja*, a traditional flank steak dish, originally introduced by the Spanish in Cuba, was appropriately named, given its close resemblance to shredded rags, featured a combination of carrot, green pepper, sweet peas, garlic cloves, some tomatoes, a couple of onions, a dash of paprika, pepper, oregano, cumin and garlic salt. Served on top of white rice, the meal was complete. Alex's mouth watered as she continued sipping her wine.

Suddenly, another bolt of lightening lit up the street as the door opened and a tall stranger headed for the bar, shaking the raindrops from his jacket. He sat down and, at once, turned to stare at Alex.

She continued to sip at her wine, as her heart raced uncontrollably. It couldn't be. Her eyes must have been playing tricks. Alex swallowed long and hard as she stared at the dark-haired man leaning over the bar and whispering into the maitre d's ear. The older man's smile widened as he hurried through the curtains behind the bar.

Then, the tall stranger rose purposefully, with the grace of a panther, and headed towards her table. Alex drank the remainder of the wine and poured herself another.

"A beautiful woman should never drink alone," he said as he slid into the chair opposite her.

A shiver went up Alex's spine. Was she hallucinating?

"You turn up in the most interesting places," she replied, gripping her glass.

The maitre d' returned with a bottle of 1982 Chateau Lafite Rothschild, showing the label to the stranger who nodded his approval.

"If you drink, you should only drink the best, and this Bordeaux will do nicely," he said, raising his glass. "Ziveli! To life!"

Alex just stared, her heart racing. This was the same man who was at the retirement home on the day of the bombing. "Who are you?"

He smiled, his black eyes pierced her already damaged armor. "*Cekaj duso*. Patience, my dear. You need time to understand. And have an open heart."

He waved at the maitre d' to bring the check. A $500 bottle of wine and he was skipping out? Alex was totally confused.

"You enjoy your dinner," he told her. "Unfortunately, I have a previous engagement. We will meet again."

He reached into his pocket for a roll of bills, counted out six hundreds. Pushing his chair back, he reached for her hand, turned the palm up and kissed the inside of her hand. "*Dovidenja, prijatno*." Goodbye and have a pleasant evening.

Alex watched as he walked out the door into the stormy night. Okay, this was too much. What the hell was going on? Her low blood sugar level must be playing tricks with her mind.

She finished her glass of wine, waving to the confused maitre d' as she ran out the door. The downpour drenched her in a few seconds. Looking left then right, she saw no one. The street was deserted.

Alex then jumped in her car and raced towards Washington Avenue where she stopped to momentarily stare at the Municipal Court building across the street. The modern structure stood like an obscene contemporary art object, cold, angular, colorful, devoid of history.

She suddenly felt alone.

The rain continued to pummel her windshield as she continued to drive home, running stop lights along the way. Pulling into her driveway, she ran to her apartment, rummaging through her rain-soaked purse for her keys. Once inside, she slammed the door shut, locking the top lock. And then, a wave of fear ran up her spine as she realized she was not alone. Someone grabbed her around the waist. Alex screamed as she turned.

"God dammit, Jason!"

"What's up, babe? I'm sorry I scared you," he said laughing, stroking her wet hair off her face, trying to make nice.

"Oh, Jason." Alex threw herself into his arms, kissing him passionately, running her tongue into his mouth, hungry for comfort. "I need to feel safe."

"Jesus, Alex. I'm sorry. The game wasn't that important," he whispered as he nibbled on her ear and began running his tongue down her neck.

Reaching for his shirt, she yanked it over his head and rubbed her cheek against his chest at the same time reaching down and slowly running her fingers along the inside of his thighs.

He groaned as he picked her up, kissing her neck, nuzzling his face between her breasts. Jason walked to the bedroom with Alex enveloped in his arms, savoring her sweet smell, licking her hot, wet skin.

Gently laying her on top of the comforter, he ran his fingers along her face. "You're so beautiful," he murmured as he unbuttoned her silk blouse and caressed her breasts, lowering his mouth to her erect nipples. Kissing and teasing, he undid the front clasp of her bra with his teeth. Lifting her pelvis, she called to him with her dark, tanned body. His hand outlined the slight but evident curves of her hips as he lowered his mouth to lick her navel. Alex pushed him back and stared at his chiselled torso. She ran her fingers down his chest, circling his nipples, and then, abruptly, unclipped his belt. He rose and removed his khaki pants and his Calvin Klein underwear, exposing muscular thighs. He wanted her.

Under her white, cotton slacks, Alex wore no underwear. She stood staring at him, then descended to meet his awaiting hand. She cradled his body, rocking slowly, tantalizing, sucking on his lower lip. He rose to meet her and entered her slowly. Alex groaned and threw her head back as she felt him penetrate. He was inside her, moving slowly, taking his time.

Jason rose, cradling her as she wrapped her legs tightly around his hips. "This is so good," he whispered moving faster, his hot breath brushing her face with every thrust as their carnal dance intensified. She bit into his shoulder as he moaned. Nothing existed except the moment, the connection, the feeling of oneness.

Alex was so close. She lifted her head in ecstasy and then screamed. A silhouetted figure stood by the window, watching.

"Oh yes, baby! Yes!" screamed Jason as he continued to thrust.

Fear and shock rippled through her body as she stared at the window. "Jason, oh my God!"

"Yes, baby! That's it, yes! Oh my God!" Jason threw his head back and shuddered as he reached orgasm, falling on top of her, kissing her passionately. Alex squirmed, trying to wriggle out from under the weight of his body.

"Look! The window!" She dug her nails into his back.

"Alex, that hurts!" cried out Jason.

"Get off of me!" She reached under his chest and flung him off the bed.

"God dammit, Alex. I was really trying this time. What the hell is wrong with you?"

"Jason, the window! There's someone there!"

"What are you nuts?" he said as he sat on the floor, rubbing his shoulder. Rising, he walked to the window, yanked at the venetian blinds and threw open the balcony door. A warm, wet wind blew into the room. The rain had stopped. A ficus tree swayed back and forth in the clay planter on the balcony. No one was there.

"For Chrissakes, Alex. You're seeing things." Jason closed the door and headed back to bed.

Alex sat there softly sobbing, her hands covering her face, as Jason's eyes softened. He quickly hopped on the bed and took her into his arms.

"Honey, it's okay. I'm sorry. Don't cry. Jesus, I hate when you cry," he said as he rocked her back and forth. "I guess you've had a couple of hard days. I'm sorry about the game." He stroked her head.

Alex lifted her tear soaked face. "It's not the game." She rolled into a small ball and curled more tightly into Jason's embrace. "Don't go home. Stay with me, okay?'

"I'm not going anywhere." He continued to stroke her head as she whimpered, slowly dropping off into a restless slumber.

The rain dripped off the roof, plopping into pools of water on the balcony. Jason hugged Alex even closer, listening to her labored breathing and the intermittent drops that lulled him to sleep.

Poor sweet, crazy Alex, thought Jason. The war in her heart needed more than a temporary truce. He closed his eyes, smiled, and then imagined himself dunking the winning shot in front of thousands of adoring fans as he drifted off to sleep.

CHAPTER TWELVE
SEE NO EVIL

"They talk about humanity as though they just invented it."

Dorothy Parker

Agent Sommett sat at his desk, staring out the window, wrapped in thought. The recent bombings had put a real glitch in his investigation and now he had to manage the fallout. One wrong move and the whole operation could blow up in his face. After years of tracking the men of Operation Bloodstone, his superiors had put a "hold" order on the investigation, and now a small-time assassin was taking his targets out one at a time. Something didn't make sense.

He had four old men, all killed within days of each other, all members of a clandestine Nazi group responsible for arms smuggling around the world. After years of trying to track their secret network, he had gathered enough evidence to link them with a covert international arms organization. First the government backed off, and now this.

Sommett was the FBI's wonderboy. As the youngest child of nine, he had grown up in poverty in the ghettos of Miami. As valedictorian and president of his high school graduating class, his SAT scores had landed him a scholarship at New York University where he had studied criminal justice. At graduation, he had been recruited by the FBI as part of their Affirmative Action policy, and proving to be a wonderful candidate, he had risen through the ranks, finally landing a cushy job in his hometown. His superiors respected him for his ardent commitment to justice and his ability to execute orders without a hitch. He was one of the best. Accomplished, smart and determined, Agent Sommett had built a reputation throughout the Justice Department for his keen investigative skills, his bravery and his loyalty.

Now Sommett's gaze focused on the Freedom Tower, a few blocks from his office building, a relic of man's never-ending battle for self-determination, for freedom. So many newly landed immigrants had once walked through the doors of that tower, seeking asylum, placing their faith in the hands of a land born of diversity, born of strife and ultimately born of the liberation of enslaved people repressed by ideology, religion or opportunity. He needed to preserve the tenets of the Constitution and he was committed to his charge.

The phone rang as he tried to refocus on his mission.

"Well, well, Agent Sommett. Miss me yet?" asked Alex, tauntingly.

"Oh, Jesus. What now?" asked Sommett, rolling his eyes. She was the proverbial thorn in his side.

"Did you read my piece this morning?"

"Unfortunately, there's only one paper worth a crap in this town. How could I miss your front-page garbage?' responded Sommett as he shuffled through his files.

"Fair enough. But, I protected my source, as promised," Alex continued.

Sommett picked up a large manila envelope and opened it. Reaching inside, he pulled out four identical red stone rings and carefully placed them, one next to the other, on the desk. He responded to Alex with silence.

"I know you're probably taping this," she continued, her voice rising an octave, "but I don't care."

Alex possessed her mother's implacable will and an undefinable inner strength that challenged the confines of acceptable behavior. Like a raw nerve, she reacted vociferously, reacting to any negative stimuli that threatened her moral or constitutional fiber. She shot straight from the hip and he respected that.

"What do you want, Alex?" Sommett asked, toying with the rings laid out on the table. He had expected her call. Throw an enticing treat to a hound and she'll come back howling for more.

"You know what I want," Alex said quickly, a sudden edge in her voice. "I'm not in the mood to play games. I can't find anything on Bloodstone. My research people have come up with zip and all the Freedom of Information Act bullshit has hit a brick wall. It's all classified. If you're planning on sending me on some wild goose chase, it's not going to work."

The FBI agent sat back in his chair and sighed. He had her where he wanted her. She was such easy prey. "How'd you sleep last night," asked Sommett, his question aimed at striking a delicate cord. This was psychological warfare.

"Look, I don't know what you're trying to get at, but as far as I'm concerned, seeing a dead body is not a daily occurrence. And, seeing a headless and handless corpse is horror movie stuff," Alex answered gruffly. "So, to answer your question, Agent Sommett, I slept just fine, given the circumstances."

"And, if I'm not going to get anywhere with you, why don't you just stop? I'm tired, and to be perfectly honest, I'm scared."

Sommett sat up and listened, his interest peaked.

"If you're not going to help me ..." she continued.

"Alex, what do you mean you're scared?" the agent asked loudly, louder than he intended. "Slow down and start over." His voice lowered to its usual level.

"I think ... I'm not sure ... God, I must be out of my mind, but I think I'm being followed," admitted Alex, her shallow breath confirming his suspicion.

"Okay, I'll tell you what," Sommett said as he gathered his files together. "Meet me at the Bimini Bar and Restaurant in one hour. Maybe we can help each other out."

Sommett knew she was on to the mystery assassin or he was on to her. As much as he hated to admit it, he needed Alex and she definitely needed him. Otherwise she had a snowball's chance in hell of getting out of this story alive.

"The damsel in distress routine always works, doesn't it," joked Alex, embarrassed by her admission. She couldn't let him get the upper hand but she did need to play him, let him think he's the alpha dog. "No more wild goose chases, okay, Sommett?"

"I never sent you on one. You're flying around the perimeter without a way of getting in. Maybe, just maybe, I'll slip you the key," said the agent as he hung up the phone.

He looked down on his desk and picked up the four rings, examining the opaque, blood-red stones. Carefully, he slid them on the index, middle and ring fingers of his right hand and stared at the carved eagles proudly clenching the Iron Cross. How many papers had been signed by the hands wearing these rings, papers sending thousands to their death? Murder by memorandum and their conscience was clean?

They might have escaped prosecution but they couldn't escape their destiny. Now four old Nazis were dead and the assassin was still out there. Agent Sommett needed to stop the killing, at least for the time being, and Alex unknowingly was going to lead him to the killer.

Wednesday at one o'clock in the afternoon, the restaurant was full of patrons dressed in tank tops, shorts and flip flops, sipping margaritas, and swaying to the Jamaican reggae beat. *Did anyone ever work in Miami,* Alex wondered as she arrived in her sleek beige pant suit. The maitre d' seated her under a palm tree with a direct view of Biscayne Bay and the dock where million dollar yachts rocked in their moorings. She fidgeted as she looked for Agent Sommett, lighting a cigarette to alleviate the tension.

He had appeared on time, dressed in khaki pants and a white t-shirt, wearing black Ray Ban sunglasses and carrying a manila envelope. He was definitely handsome, tall with broad shoulders and strong, athletic legs. His gleaming white smile could melt the hardest of hearts, but Alex knew better. He was as calculating as they come; she had to play his game and play it well.

"Good to see you again," he said as he pulled out a cushioned wicker chair and sat down, slowly placing the envelope on the seat next to Alex.

She eyed the envelope on the chair, ready to pounce. How was she supposed to react? All this clandestine stuff was beyond her.

The FBI agent sensed her apprehension. "Just act normal. Don't do anything out of the ordinary. We're two friends having lunch, okay?" He offered her the menu.

Alex nodded, took it and smiled benignly. "I'm not used to playing undercover," she told him, her tone mildly defensive.

"You're doing fine," he said, smiling his first smile of the day. "Just follow my cues and we'll be off and running."

As they perused the menu, their Caribbean waiter swaggered over and asked for their orders in a distinct, lyrical Jamaican accent.

"Hey, man, what's up?" Sommett said immediately as he shook the waiter's hand. He was really good at his cover. No one would have suspected that this thirty-something, gorgeous black man was an FBI agent and not a model on South Beach, posing during the day for catalogue work and partying at night in the clubs. He was a nineties version of Miami Vice, cool, unapproachable and self-absorbed.

"The swordfish sandwich is great here," Sommett said as he eyed the menu. "What are you in the mood for, baby girl?"

"A coffee please," answered Alex, amazed by Sommett's cool demeanor. He was good, really good.

"Not a single woman eats in this town. What is up with that?" he retorted, shaking his head as he placed his menu down. "Give me a woman with something to grab onto."

The waiter smiled broadly as slapped Sommett's hand in true high five fashion. "You're so right, *mon*."

"A bacon cheeseburger, please, medium rare with grilled onions, fries and a coke," Sommett ordered, smacking his lips.

Alex sat there, speechless. He unnerved her and she hated not having the upper hand. "So, Agent Sommett," she said, resting her chin in her hand and smiling seductively. "You like a woman with a little bit of meat on her bones?"

"You need to feed the mind in order for it to function properly," responded Sommett nonchalantly, ignoring her blatant attempts at flirtation. "Maybe that's been your problem. You're not eating right." Clearly he was amused and not prepared to buy into her game.

Alex sat back in her chair, pouting. "Spare me the pseudo concern," she said, her face more flushed by the minute. "I eat just fine and my mind is perfectly clear and functioning, thank you. Besides, I have plenty of men who find me desirable."

"No offense," answered Sommett coolly.

"None taken."

"Suit yourself," he said, not paying her much attention.

They stared at the beams of light reflecting off the tiny ripples of waves in the bay. Three pelicans sat perched on wooden posts by the water, spreading their wings to dry them in the scorching heat.

Alex watched him as his eyes darted left and right behind his sunglasses, analyzing the perimeter for any formidable threat. Obviously, Sommett was a predator. Always on alert, he had finely tuned radar that kept him alive all these years. It seemed to her that he was seconds from drawing his government issued semi-automatic pistol adhered to his bulging calf muscle. Alex relaxed, reluctantly accepting the momentary safety zone. He was so strong, so assured, so capable, so much a man. She liked that, yet she knew she couldn't trust a governmental bone in his body.

"So, what do you have for me?" asked Alex, fondling the envelope on the seat beside her.

"Stay still," ordered Sommett as he removed his sunglasses. He glared menacingly at her. Alarmed, Alex quickly recoiled.

"What's wrong?" she asked, frightened not so much by his words as by the rancor in his voice.

"You really are an amateur, aren't you?" admonished the agent. "You're not to open it here. This isn't a game. The faster you get that through your head, the better. I'm sharing a top secret document with you and you're treating it like I just handed you some recent head shots."

He continued with his instructions. "When we say goodbye, you will enjoy a walk around the docks and then slowly go to your car. You will examine the documents at home and then you will put them in a safe deposit box. No one else is to see them. Understood?"

Alex turned beet red as the blood rushed to her cheeks, feeling like a five-year-old who had just been scolded by her father. "I'm sorry," she said dejectedly, shaking her head with grim assurance. "Patience isn't one of my virtues."

"Look, I want to help you but you better get with the program," he told her, without hesitation. "Follow my instructions to the letter. If you don't, you're on your own, and let me tell you something, all the bravado you can muster up won't save your ass. Understood?"

Alex feebly nodded her head, accepting the terms of their partnership.

"Good. I'm expecting you to be a quick study. After all, you're a pretty bright woman. Don't disappoint me. Smile. Look at me and laugh. Act as though we're old friends." Sommett smiled as he reached for her hand and squeezed hard. He almost crushed her fingers in his grasp.

Alex forced a smile and leaned in. "Why all this cloak and dagger stuff?"

"You said you were being followed. And if you are, then I'm sure he's not too far away. You don't want to end up floating in Biscayne Bay, do you?"

Alex recoiled as she looked around the restaurant. "Do you think he's here?"

"If he's a pro, then you won't know when or where he's lurking. Just be assured that he's keeping you under 24-7. I'm not sure who he is but he obviously needs something from you so you're safe as long as he still thinks you're of some value," he said matter-of-factly.

Alex reached for another cigarette, struggling to light it in the brisk breeze coming off the bay. Her mind was spinning. It was as though she was watching herself in some bizarre movie.

"Welcome to the big leagues," said Sommett with a crafty wink. "Are you sure you're ready to play?"

"I don't know what I'm getting myself into," answered Alex, exhaling a dense cloud of smoke and slowly sipping her coffee, trying to keep her hand from shaking.

"It's more than you ever bargained for. Read the file," said Sommett. "Alex, I will protect you," the agent said soothingly. "Trust me."

Famous last words. This time she didn't have much of a choice. "My life is in your hands," she said, looking him straight in the eye.

"You're learning, baby girl," he told her, nodding his head. "You're learning."

CHAPTER THIRTEEN
THE WINGS OF TIME

"It's a sad and stupid thing to have to proclaim yourself a revolutionary just to be a decent man."
David Harris

It was nearly four when Alex finally left Agent Sommett at the restaurant with the file safely tucked in her purse. She roamed around the docks after their meeting, and watched the pelicans crash land in the choppy bay, surfacing with flapping fish in their beaks. *They are so awkward*, thought Alex as she watched the giant birds gulp down their catch of the day. She caught a glimpse of the ominous sky, and saw an afternoon thunderstorm approaching. It was time to head home and read the documents. The dark sky was quickly approaching and threatened to open up and swallow her whole as she drove across the Venetian Causeway.

Alex arrived ten minutes later and ran up the exposed stairwell to her apartment just as it started pouring. By the time she reached the top of the landing, she was soaking wet. Locking the double lock behind her, she threw her purse on the couch. She then darted to the big sliding glass doors and drew the curtains closed before checking in every closet and under the bed in case the phantom assassin was sitting there waiting to pounce. Alex wasn't taking any chances.

Lightening flashed behind the closed curtains as a violent crack of thunder shook the building. Alex shivered as she removed her drenched clothes and put on a thick terry cloth robe. She headed to the kitchen and picked up a kettle to boil water.

Nazis?

Alex shook her head in disbelief. There's no way.

She turned off the stove and opened the freezer and pulled out a half-empty bottle of vodka. Forget the tea. She needed to soothe her nerves.

Alex poured herself a glass of the clear liquor, walked into her living room and reached for the file in her purse. The vodka warmed her insides as she reached over, opened the file and started to read.

To her amazement, Alex found herself flipping through a series of black and white photographs of young SS officers proudly standing side-by-side, and valiantly staring into the camera lens. The caption read "Jasenovac 1941 - 1945 — Colonel Wilhelm Heidrich, General Joseph Gruntler, Captain Fritz Schmidt, Captain Eric Klempner, Captain Hans Gotsfried, Captain Dieter Heidrich and Captain Hermann Heidrich."

Continuing to riffle through the file, she found a secret government document labeled "Operation Bloodstone"—CIA Report 1946-1950. Alex couldn't believe her eyes. Apparently, American intelligence had helped bring these Nazi fugitives over after WWII, hoping to harness the knowledge of the Third Reich before it fell into Russian hands. Everything was done in the name of anti-communism during the early Cold War years.

She knew that right before the end of the war, both British and American intelligence teams had sifted through the cadre of scientific and military personnel, particularly those whose work had nearly won the war for Germany, hoping to scoop up an intelligence jewel in the carnage. Their work was meticulous and purposeful. But, there was one problem—it was illegal.

The original model for the Iran-Contra affair was created decades ago with Operation Bloodstone, as the U.S. government felt justified in breaking the law in the name of national interest. As Alex continued to dig deeper into the documents in front of her, she saw history repeating itself over and over again.

She had read that, although United States law specifically prohibited Nazi officials from emigrating to America, as many as seventy-five percent of those considered for entry were committed Nazis. Most were rejected but the few that had entered and stayed had done so with the aid of the government. It was a tradeoff. A few Nazis in exchange for vital information about the USSR. At the end of WWII, the United States became involved in a new war, a war against Stalin, and they were prepared to win at any price.

Just like with Operation Paperclip and Operation Ratlines, which grabbed the best German scientific minds right before the war ended, U.S. intelligence smuggled core German planners and intelligence officers out before the Russians got their hands on them.

Highly educated and experienced in Eastern Europe, the Bloodstone members were part of that secret roundup. These German spymasters packed microfilmed records of the USSR in watertight steel drums, and secretly buried them in a remote mountain meadow in Bosnia.

In the spring of 1945, General Joseph Gruntler negotiated a new life for his elite SS group stationed in Croatia including Gottsfried, Schmidt, Klempner and the Heidrich brothers. He exchanged the drums for their lives and safe passage. The U.S. secretly agreed, banking on using their knowledge of the Balkans to stop the spread of communism which threatened to infest every country west of the Russian front.

The Bloodstone members were funneled out through transit camps and were issued phony passports along with an estimated 5,000 other Nazis who left Europe and relocated around the world. Their immigration files were rewritten to eliminate incriminating evidence of Nazi references. Their dossiers were quickly cleared and immediately reflected security evaluations stating, "No incriminating information is available on the subject ... it is the opinion of the Military Governor that he may not constitute a security threat to the United States."

Most of the fleeing Nazis went to South and Central America where some, like Klaus Barbie, helped governments set up death squads in Argentina, El Salvador, and Chile.

Alex continued flipping through the pages, her heart racing, skipping a beat as she delved further and further into the document. Why had Sommett given her this report? Clearly, the evidence was not only embarrassing to the United States but was morally reprehensible. And, what did the agent have to gain by leaking these papers to the press and possibly compromising his position at the FBI? Alex continued her investigation and opened another document— "Brand Industries and National Security Interests."

The report highlighted the formation of the arms and ammunitions conglomerate, and outlined its intrinsic yet clandestine ties to the U.S. government. Like the other transplanted Germans, the members of Bloodstone had focused on investing their portion of the 350 million Swiss francs held in the Vatican for safekeeping. Some fifty million francs of the Nazi gold which ended up in the bank accounts of the Heidrich brothers had been used to finance the lifestyle of the fleeing Nazis, as well as enable them to form Brand Industries and, ironically enough, begin contributing to the gross national product of the United States.

As these documents proved, Wilhelm Heidrich had established one of the most profitable guns and ammunitions cartels in America, employing thousands, and padding the pockets of numerous, influential investors. He had become a Who's Who of the corporate world, contributing to both Democratic and Republican coffers, dazzling Wall Street with record breaking earnings and seducing greedy investors with huge profits.

Alex sat back, perplexed at the hypocrisy. On the one hand, the United States had made a pact with these men years ago, an arrangement that could cast shame on the country, and on the other, they were presently breaking current laws, orchestrating a vast arms smuggling network, providing guns and ammunition to terrorist organizations including the IRA and some Middle East groups supported by the likes of Moammar Khadaffi and Osama Bin Laden.

Clearly the U.S. was not only fully aware of the international arms smuggling, but was willing to condone it if the arms were being shipped to a group currently listed on the government's "A" list. The problem was that the list was constantly updated. If the freedom fighters of the month promised to support the United States' vital interests in the warring region, then they got the green light. If not, they were considered "enemies of the state." The duplicity was simple. Washington was prepared to foot the bill, throw up smoke screens and fully arm the insurgents if, and only if, they followed orders dished out by Pennsylvania Avenue. And, the United States had built up quite an arsenal of enemies around the world due to its clandestine policies. Every attempt to control the world's hot pockets produced a whole new bunch of angry extremists with a single mission—revenge against America for broken promises and backstabbing.

Alex threw the report on the couch and reached for the bottle, pouring the remainder of the vodka in her glass. Where did you draw the line? Terrorists or freedom fighters? It was a matter of interpretation and the interpretation was determined by whether or not the U.S. was going to come out on top.

Alex knew that whatever Brand Industries was currently involved in infringed on delicate diplomatic territory and had to do with the war in Yugoslavia, a region that was currently in turmoil.

Croatia had just recently normalized relations with Iran, and its first ambassador was working out the details of a clandestine weapons pipeline to supply Bosnia's vulnerable Muslim army.

The U.S. just won the Persian Gulf War, and needed to make diplomatic amends to the Muslim world. It was feared that any scandal involving the scapegoating of another Muslim group might seriously damage the delicate balance of diplomacy.

Although the international arms embargo was in place, the U.S. administration was turning a blind eye to complex arms shipments from Iran and Turkey as well as from U.S. allies as Pakistan, Malaysia, Saudi Arabia and Argentina. Alex realized that Brand Industries had to have its greedy fingers in on the arms mother lode.

No wonder they were trying to bump people off! Millions of dollars and the New World Order were at stake. Alex's head began to spin. How the hell had she become involved in this mess? Maybe Agent Sommett was right. She should stick to her clean little world.

Alex walked back into the living room and reached for the phone. She called her mother.

"Hi, Mom. What are you doing?"

"Come for dinner. I have a lovely cheese *gibanica* in the oven," said Zvona, tempting her with the filla dough, cheese-filled Balkan delicacy.

"How did you know that's what I need?" Alex asked her.

"I'm your mother."

Alex smiled. "I'll be there in ten." She grabbed her purse after closing the file and hiding it under the couch.

The rain had stopped and a rainbow formed a multi-colored arch over Miami Beach. Alex drove her car onto Pine Tree Drive, the beautiful tree-lined road just west of the canal, dividing Miami Beach into interconnected peninsulas, a stone's throw from the wide beaches and the Atlantic Ocean.

Her mother's home was an old Spanish-style house on the corner of a cul-de-sac, bordering a canal. Alex pulled into the circular driveway as Zvona opened the front door, holding her arms out to her only progeny.

"Glad to see that you dressed for the occasion," she said, as she critically eyed Alex's tattered sweat suit. "Such a lovely color on you—black."

"Please don't start, Mom. I've had a hard day."

Alex gave her mother a kiss as she walked through the door, threw her things down on the big armchair in the hallway, and observed balefully.

"Don't ask. Okay?"

Zvona shot her daughter a steaming glare as Alex pulled out the slivovitz from the kitchen cabinet.

"Haven't you had enough?" she asked as she checked the *gibanica* in the oven.

"Can we talk, Mom? " responded Alex as she poured herself a stiff shot and sat down at the kitchen counter. "I'd like to know about Daddy."

Zvona stiffened and closed the oven door. "Well then, pour me a shot, too. A good one."

She groaned as she sat beside her daughter. Zvona didn't smoke cigarettes, but took one out of Alex's pack anyway.

"Okay. What's this all about," she demanded, coughing slightly as she exhaled.

"I'd just like to know some things. About Daddy. About how you guys ever hooked up. You know what I mean—you're Croatian and he was Serbian."

Zvona downed the last of the slivovitz and pointed at the glass for another shot. "Back then, we were all Yugoslavs, or so I thought," she explained. "Actually, I wonder if there ever was a true Yugoslavia. My family was always Croatian and your father's family was always Serbian, but we all lived under Tito's communist rule. There wasn't much of a choice. We were never Yugoslavs just subjects of Yugoslavia."

"So, what am I?"

"You're my daughter, and I love you," responded her mother with pride.

"So, I'm just part of a category of children from ethnically mixed marriages who lack ethnic identity?"

Zvona shook her head. "You're a beautiful child who grew into a beautiful woman. You have so much compassion, *macane*, perhaps too much."

Alex reached over and patted her mother's hand. "The fruit doesn't fall far from the tree."

Zvona smiled then stared out the kitchen window.

"It was so different back then, wasn't it?" Alex asked her.

"I suppose so," she answered, turning to face her daughter.

Alex was aware that back in the 1800s, groups of educated Serbs, Croats and Slovenes wanted to unify all South Slavs in order to free themselves from foreign domination, namely the Turks and the Austrians, and it was only after the first World War that such a union become reality. Yugoslavia officially was formed in 1921, and Serbian King Aleksandar I Karadjordjevic became the king of Yugoslavia. It was much like what Kaiser Wilhelm I did when he was the emperor of Germany, or Vittorio Emmanuel did as the king of Italy, but the German and Italian people agreed to have more in common than not, unlike the South Slavs. Yugoslavia was torn from the beginning between the more numerous and already politically independent Serbs and the more

Westernized Croats and Slovenes. Therefore, Aleksandar's kingdom was doomed from the start as the Croats and Slovenes envisioned creating not a single country but more of a confederacy in which they would get full statehood.[4]

"So, was the union always fragile?" Alex asked her, her eyes bright and wild with curiosity. "Was there ever a true Yugoslavia?"

"No, I'm afraid not," her mother replied somberly.

"So what do we do now?" she asked, after a breath.

"We pray that they don't all kill each other in the name of nationalism," Zvona said at last, weariness in her voice.

"So who's right and who's wrong?" Alex asked. "It seems as though everyone's confused."

"That's not surprising," replied Zvona, without hesitation. "The public needs to see a good guy and a bad guy, and these characters can't alternate places on a daily basis. It's just too much for the general public. One day it's Serbs who flee from burned villages, the next day it's Croats, and a few days later it's Muslims. Who's chasing whom away? In what part of the country? For what reason? The problem comes in when there's so much information that should be shared in the name of truth, but only minutes of airtime to do it in. Journalists are paid to *oversimplify* complex situations. We're bombarded by nothing but Orwellian newspeak and doubletalk, both of which by the way, is coming from official government sources and high paid PR firms."

Zvona continued the history lesson explaining that the war in Bosnia in 1992 was not only due to external aggression against a territory, but was also fueled by irreconcilable political differences between ethnic communities. The Muslims wanted to claim the state as their own and dominate the other two groups. The Serbs wanted to keep Bosnia-Hercegovina in Yugoslavia and secede to form a separate state once that goal was no longer practical, while the Croats' ultimate aim was annexation of their ethnic territories to Croatia proper. All those people caught in between, or left behind, were given three choices—become a disenfranchised minority with limited rights, move away, or die.[5]

From the beginning, Bosnia never actually had independence except for a medieval kingdom whose population had virtually no cultural or national resemblance to the present inhabitants. Like the rest of the Mediterranean region, Bosnia at that time was part of the Roman Empire, and after the fall of Rome became an area contested between Byzantium and Rome's successors in the West. By the 7th century AD, Bosnia was settled by Slavs, and by the 9th century saw the establishment of the kingdoms of Serbia, and Croatia. During the 11th and 12th centuries, Bosnia was governed by local nobles under the authority of the Kings of Hungary and around 1200 A.D., Bosnia fought for and gained its independence. The Kingdom of Bosnia endured some 260 years.[6]

Thereafter, Bosnia has always been a province or territory of some empire, whether Turkish, Austrian or otherwise, and its modern history has been mostly marred in bloodshed as evidenced in 1914, 1941 and 1992.

During the most recent Balkan war, many accused that the dispute among the Bosnian Muslims, Croats and Serbs had been used to promote the agenda of none other than the United States. From the beginning of the 1990s, Bosnia was considered as the linchpin of America's foreign policy in the region, and the United States was accused of sabotaging peace efforts and fueling the conflict. To make matters worse, those same accusers believed the United States then used the deadly turmoil to promote its role as supposed peacemaker and security insurer of post-Cold War Europe. In the process, NATO was reborn. The nearly obsolete Cold War relic once again became an aggressive military alliance with a mission, accumulating more power and responsibility in the area.[7]

Bosnia exemplified the depth of the Balkans curse, and it also represented a tragedy the United States could not begin to fathom, no matter which administration held power in Washington.[8]

"The hatreds are so deeply rooted, *macane*. They go back centuries," Zvona said, her eyes worried. "The Serbs have been so heavy-handed with their desire to form a Greater Serbia, but I can't say that the Muslims or the Croats have been much better with their own nationalistic desires to form their own. The big difference is that one side has all the guns."

"So, what do we do? Arm them all and see who comes out on top?" asked Alex, a hysterical edge in her voice.

"That would be an easy solution," continued Zvona, with no attempt at irony. "On the one hand, how can we stand by and watch one side slaughter another? On the other, I'm not sure the less armed Muslims and Croats wouldn't do the same if they had the upper hand. Throw in a bunch of nationalistic hoodlums and leaders only concerned with their own legacy and mired in their own self interests, and you have the Bosnian situation in a nutshell."

"Did all this matter when you married *tata*?"

"Nothing really matters all that much when you have love," replied her mother, struggling to hold back her tears.

Zvona reached over and took Alex into her arms, hugging her tightly. "Let's eat," she said finally. "Good food soothes all our demons."

Alex agreed and poured another glass of slivovitz as she watched the sun set through the big veranda glass doors. The gentle wind blew the bougainvillea branches against the patio. Her mother removed the *gibanica* from the oven and began setting the table.

Alex walked to the patio doors and opened them, letting in the late day breeze. *I'm just a Balkan mutt,* thought Alex as she watched the horizon slowly shrink, acquiescing to the evening sky. Tears welled up in her dark eyes.

Misha sat hidden in the early evening shadows, watching, having followed Alex from the restaurant to her apartment, and finally to her mother's house where he had sneaked into the backyard and hid behind the big areca palms.

There was something about this woman that intrigued and excited him. He walked to the patio as Alex retreated into the kitchen. For the last hour, he had sat watching her and her mother through the big bay window. His heart ached. He needed to know what was in the file, but more than that, he needed to know Alex.

A gentle early evening breeze blew in from the Atlantic as Alex hugged her mother goodbye and promised to call her the next day. Driving across the 41st Street bridge, she parked her car at the entrance to the beach.

The sun had set behind her, the final remains of the day flickering between the highrise buildings. Alex took her shoes off and walked onto the beach, feeling the grains of sand oozing through her toes. She sat at the edge of the Atlantic and stared at the glistening ocean waves breaking on shore. The water was as smooth as glass. Not a wave rippled in the aftermaths of the afternoon storm.

"*Duso, kazi mi,*" said a deep voice from behind her. Talk to me.

Alex stiffened in fright, dread crawling up her spine like a cold hand. She turned to face Misha.

"This is getting a bit freaky," responded Alex, a petulant edge to her voice, as she turned back to face the ocean, her cheeks burning. "The other night you bought me a very expensive bottle of wine and then disappeared. Now you're showing up on a deserted beach, asking me to reveal my soul."

Misha sat beside her and put his jean jacket over her shoulders. "The weather's going to turn."

Alex nodded as she wrapped it around her and breathed in the pungent, masculine smell.

"I lost my mother when I was young," volunteered Misha. "You're lucky to have her."

Suddenly Alex's heart lurched as fear ran up her spine. She threw the jacket off her shoulders and started bolting across the beach for the parking lot. Misha followed and tackled her in the sand. They rolled around for a couple of rounds and Alex ended up pinned, a couple of inches from his unshaven face.

"You leave her alone," cried Alex, trembling in earnest.

"I don't want to hurt you or your mother, Alexandra. Please, just hear me out," he pleaded as he released the pressure on her arms. He helped her sit up and brushed the sand from her hair.

"If you're going to kill me then just go ahead and do it," she whispered, her eyes as lightless as stone.

"Kill you? What are you talking about?"

"What were you doing at the bombing scenes?" asked Alex as she moved a few inches away from him. "Did you kill those old men?"

"*Srce moje*. My heart. Do you know who those men were?"

"Yes," answered Alex, nodding half-heartedly.

"I just wanted to bring them to justice," sighed Misha. "For fifty years they escaped punishment. They killed my family," he said as he slowly laid back on the sandy beach, his arms behind his head, staring at the dark sky.

"Did you kill them?" Alex asked him again, raising the fine hairs on her head.

"No."

Alex couldn't believe her eyes or ears. Here she was, sitting on a deserted South Florida beach with a gorgeous terrorist of some kind, swapping stories and rolling in the warm sand. For a moment, she felt like she was going to lose her mind.

"What the hell do you want with me?" Alex asked, calmly as possible.

"I need your help."

"I can't help you. I can't even help myself," said Alex as she started to cry. The fatigue was bringing her emotions to a boil.

"*Nemoj, duso.*" Don't cry. He wrapped his arms around Alex and held her.

"I don't understand what is happening. Why am I involved in this mess?"

"Maybe it's your legacy," Misha said as he gently stroked her hair. "Will you hear me out?"

Alex nodded and handed him the keys to her car. They drove to her apartment and closed the door to the outside world. Alex went into the kitchen and came out with a bottle of *slivovitz*. She placed the bottle and two shot glasses on the coffee table.

"Ziveli!" said Misha as he threw the first shot down his parched throat.

"How can you drink to life?" asked Alex, shaking her head.

"Can you think of something better to wish for?"

"I suppose not." Alex sipped the clear plum brandy and placed the glass on the floor.

He sat across from her. His beautiful chiselled Balkan features toyed with the light streaming in from the window. "How much do you know," he asked in a brusque way.

"Not much. Maybe too much," replied Alex, almost apologetically. "I just don't know."

Suddenly realizing the envelope of documents was sticking out from its hiding place beneath the couch, she quickly pushed the exposed edge back under.

"These men were killers," he told her. "Mass murderers," repeated Misha, savoring both the words and *slivovitz*. "Not only did they kill my family, they tainted the reputation of all good Croatians everywhere."

"My mother's family never supported the Nazis!" exclaimed Alex anxiously.

"I never said they did. Not all Croatians supported the *Ustashe*. Some even helped by fighting with the Partisans. I have nothing against your mother's family."

"Then what?!" cried Alex as she curled her knees into her chest, as though protecting herself from an unknown onslaught.

"The file you have contains information about men who killed hundreds of thousands during the second World War in Yugoslavia. They killed my grandfather."

"We're from two separate worlds, you and I," Alex said as she reached for the partially filled glass of the plum brandy. "I don't know of any of this."

"These men are still killing today," he replied, hostility in his voice.

"They're not pulling any triggers," she reminded him, turning away to light a cigarette, though the one she had already lit was still burning in the ashtray. "They are part of some big corporation that ships arms and ammunitions to those who want to blow each other's brains out!"

"So, you condone murder by memorandum?" he asked wryly.

"God, no!" Alex exclaimed.

"There's no difference in what they did then and what they're doing now," Misha said firmly. "Fifty years ago they charged the *Ustashe* to do their ugly dealings. Today, they're making millions while hundreds of thousands flounder to find enough ammo to blow the other side to oblivion! I can't sit here and watch that happen. Not again."

"Who are you?"

"I'm a member of a group that seeks justice."

"Is your group killing these guys?"

"Would you stand by and watch while thousands of your own were being killed?" he demanded. "Could you not pull the trigger if someone was killing your family?"

"Is that a yes?" asked Alex.

Misha didn't answer. Reaching for the file under the couch, he ransacked through the mound of papers until he found a photo of hundreds of bodies buried in a mass grave. The photo read, "Jasenovac — April 1945." He shoved the picture in front of Alex's face.

"I want justice for this," he said.

Alex covered her eyes.

Misha reached over and cupped her sorrowful face in his large hands. "Your father would have done the same," he told her, his words almost a whisper.

"No!" Alex jumped from the couch and ran for the front door. Misha cornered her against the wall in the hallway and held her as she struggled.

"Let me go!" she cried, beating on his chest.

Alex was beyond furious. How dare this small time, would be assassin compare himself with her father. No one could hold a candle to her *tata*.

"I'm not here to hurt you," Misha said, shaking her. "Open your eyes and see the truth. Tell me to go and I will," he pleaded. "Tell me you want no part of this battle and I'll leave you be."

She was mesmerized by the longing in his eyes.

He gently reached for her and pulled her close. She felt his hot breath on her neck.

"Tell me that you don't feel there is something between us—and, I won't believe you," Misha said breathlessly.

He ran his fingers along her lips then, leaned in, kissing her passionately, exploring the inside of her mouth with his tongue. His hands hungrily tore at her T-shirt, ripping the thin fabric in two, exposing her small, perfectly shaped breasts.

"*Malena.*" My little one, he whispered as he whisked her up in his arms and headed for the bedroom.

"This is wrong," Alex murmured as she kissed him back.

"*Nije ako je dobro.* It's not wrong if it's something good," Misha told her, as he laid her down on the bed and removed his shirt. Alex stared at the tattoo of the black hand on his chest. Her fingers followed the intricate design and ended at the pointed end of the knife.

"I don't even know you," she protested.

"How much do you need to know?"

Alex felt his warm body against hers.

"*Kazi mi, duso,*" he said. Talk to me. "*Pokazi mi.*" Show me.

Alex's eyes flooded with tears as he pulled her to him.

"*Dodi kuci* … come home. *Ja cu da ti pokazem* … I'll show you the way," he whispered.

Alex trembled as she kissed Misha, surrendering herself to him. Whether he was another harbinger of false promises didn't matter. This man lit the fires of her spirit.

CHAPTER FOURTEEN
DEATH BECOMES HER

"To do evil fighting evil,
In this there can be no evil."
Nyegosh of Montenegro

Alex had trouble getting to sleep. She had stayed awake most of the night as Misha lay beside her, snoozing peacefully. What had she done? Was he the killer? *He couldn't be,* she told herself. He was so gentle, so proud and full of life, and so very sad. There was something pure about him, something absolutely transparent yet inexplicably dissettling at the same time. She burned the pangs of lust into her memory.

All night she thought of him caressing her body, and taking her with such intensity. She couldn't remember the last time she had shared herself so completely. His touch had triggered something deep inside of her, exposing feelings and desires buried for so long. The intense connection between them was inexplicable.

Alex finally drifted into a deep sleep, as the sun began to rise below the horizon.

Misha woke to find her curled under the covers, soundly asleep. He rose quietly, dressed, and left without a goodbye or a farewell kiss. He had work to do.

Driving to South Beach, he walked to the hotel on 6th Street and found Vera waiting for him in the lobby.

Her wrap-around skirt fell open as she moved to make room on the couch, revealing long, muscular legs. She had the body of a finely trained athlete.

"*Kazi mi istinu,*" Vera demanded the truth as he took a seat beside her. She was a true, tall beauty with big, black eyes, an energetic smile and a temperament only a mother could love. By the looks of things, Misha had his hands full.

"The truth? My fair Serbian maiden, the truth is that yesterday I fought a great fight. I am greatly wounded and my heart is bloodless," Misha told her, quoting an old Serbian poem about the battle at Kosovo.

"That's a bunch of bullshit!"

Vera rose from the big couch and stormed by him in the direction of the door. "I'm sure Peja will want to know that you're sleeping with the enemy!"

Misha rushed to her side and grabbing her by the arms, he twisted her around to face him. "Don't be a fool. Everything I do, I do for us."

"A curse upon your soul!" she cried, pulling away from him and running out the hotel lobby.

He stopped her in the middle of Ocean Drive, creating gridlock on the busy street. The cars blared their horns as the two stood yelling at each other.

"So, you made love to that Croatian cunt?" Vera demanded.

"She's only part Croatian."

Infuriated, Vera flung a right hook, catching Misha on his left jaw. He recoiled in pain, then smiled, caressing his face.

The cars continued to honk.

"*Yebem ti*!" screamed Vera at the drivers as Misha dragged her to the sidewalk where she continued to struggle in his arms, hitting his chest and face. Misha took the beating until she tired.

"Are you done?"

"*Yebem ti,*" she whimpered, exhausted from the exchange.

He lead her back to the hotel and they entered their room, groping each other.

"A curse upon your mother, your house, and your children's souls," whispered Vera as she pulled him to the queen-size bed. "*Poljubi me,*" she added. "Kiss me."

Misha removed his T-shirt and caressed his tattoo. "Wash my brows and fill my cup with wine. I have returned from fighting the infidels," he quoted as he lowered himself on top of her.

"Damn you to hell, Misha," she muttered as she buried her anger in his ardent thrusts.

✳ ✳ ✳

Peja and the rest of the Black Hand gang were meeting at the News Café on South Beach for their daily expressos and intake of world news from the pages of the *New York Times*, *The International Herald Tribune* and *Le Monde* as Misha and Vera arrived, flushed from a morning of fighting and making up. Vera smirked as she walked by the table of the cajoling warriors.

"Vera, if your mother only knew!"

"Your mother would give her second born for a daughter-in-law like me," she retorted.

"*Sestro*, I'd give anything for one night with you," exclaimed one of the burly members. "Sister, you name the place and time."

Peja smacked the insolent soldier. "A bit of respect," he said. "She's worth more deaf, dumb and blind than all of you put together!"

"So, where the hell were you, Misha?'

Misha ordered a double shot of Cuban coffee. "I have our entrée."

"That's a *double entendre* if I ever heard one," snickered Vera, throwing her head back and laughing.

"That's enough," retorted Misha, shooting a venomous stare at his paramour.

"The woman is starting to trust me," he told the others. "I've already seen the file and I think she will do what I ask if I spend a bit more time priming her."

"Is that what we call fucking these days?" chimed Vera, throwing her napkin across the table at him.

Misha glared menacingly at her.

"*Dosta*. Okay, that's enough," Peja interjected calmly. "We don't have time for your petty jealousies."

The older man suddenly reached across the table and smacked Misha's face. "And, a bit of respect for our Vera, you hear me?"

Misha blew a kiss to Vera, whereupon she flung herself at him in a fury while the other men rose to separate them. Peja, bringing everything to a halt with a few well-chosen words, slipped the manager a hundred dollar bill and they were led to a private room inside the restaurant.

The men and Vera all took their seats calmly although she refused to sit beside Misha who, in turn, assumed an expression of self satisfaction as he took the chair in the corner, nearest the exit.

"Okay, Misha, take a walk," ordered Peja as he sat at the head of the table. "I think we've all seen enough drama for one day."

Misha rose defiantly, leaving without uttering a word while Peja corralled Vera between the table and the wall as she rose screaming on the top of her lungs.

"*Jebem ti, svinja!*" Fuck you, pig.

The gang was coming apart at the sexual seams. Peja had known this would become a problem when he formed his team back in Belgrade.

Some of them came from Vojvodina, an area of Serbia with strong nationalistic ties. Misha and Vera's families had returned to Serbia after the tensions mounted in Croatia, leaving behind a couple of decades of friendships which unfortunately separated along nationalistic lines. Their Croat neighbors formed their owned alliances, ostracizing the Serb families in Krajina.

Since he was a small child, Misha had grown up hearing of the atrocities committed during WWII. The Croatian fascists had slaughtered hundreds of thousands all in the name of this being "a good occasion for us to help Croatia save the countless souls." Those countless souls included Orthodox Serbs, Jews and Gypsies. Misha's grandfather was amongst those sacrificed, dying a horrific death at Jasenovac.

After the war, Misha's mother, Dubravka, became a confirmed communist, a Tito compatriot, even though her heart secretly belonged to the Orthodox Church, and her only son. And, she taught him well. He adored her vibrant spirit, her loving motherly arms and her inability to forget.

Their simple days together were spent plowing cornfields and harvesting plums from a nearby orchard. His father, Zoran, fermented the plums, brewing *slivovitz* in an oak drum in the barn, frequently dipping to check the recipe. Krajina, meaning "border" or "the land in between," was a Serbian enclave in the midst of Croatia and stretched 100 miles from the Adriatic to the Hungarian Border. This was where Misha had learned to love and hate.

Dubravka never forgave the death of her father. She taught her son to be self-sufficient, strong and proud of his family's sacrifice. Bedtime tales were filled with stories of brave warriors and ancient battlegrounds. When he was fifteen, his mother suddenly died of a heart attack, her sorrow too great to bear. When she died, something went haywire like an electric circuit malfunction, and Misha was never the same.

The young Serb was the first in his family not to lose a father to war. His father was a tall burly man with a delicate mental constitution. After the death of his wife and unable to stand the torment alone, he hanged himself in the back of the barn. That day, Misha was left without a family, but with a talent and spirit inherited from his grandfather. He became an assassin with a predisposition to explosives and an undying devotion to the dead.

Peja had seen this potential and had hoped to harness Misha's anger into a strident, fighting machine. He now needed to control him.

"Vera, stop your diatribe," he snapped as he read a map spread out on the table. "He's been under a lot of pressure. So far the bombings have gone off without a hitch, but the next target is the most important."

"But he's fucking her!"

"I don't care. And neither should you. If he gets us closer to our goal, then it doesn't matter."

"Bullshit! It's either him or me," exclaimed Vera.

"Don't make me choose," warned Peja.

"She's Croatian! What happened to your loyalty to our women?"

"Loyalty is to Serbian land," Peja said, pounding his fist on the table, rattling the glasses. "We will do whatever needs to be done to achieve that goal. But, listen to me, and listen to me good, I will control him as long as I know that doing so will make him effective. No more than that. Do you hear me? You will not dictate to me."

His eyes mellowed as he hugged the only female member of his brigade.

"You are our future," he told her. "You will bear our sons. We salute you. But, don't ever step over the boundary again. Support him and we will ride into the kingdom of God together!"

Vera reluctantly agreed. "If I need to sacrifice myself," she told him, her eyes downcast, her spirit temporarily bridled by loyalty, " then I will do so."

"Good," Peja said approvingly. "Now go home. He needs you."

As Vera left the rowdy group and walked along the busy oceanside street, a tall man rose from one of the tables on the outside terrace and followed her, keeping a hundred feet behind. When she entered the hotel, he sat on the bench across the street.

Aegis had found his targets.

Misha sat in the hotel room sharpening his knife with a weathered leather strap and staring out the window. She walked in and headed towards him. She started massaging his shoulders and then lowered her face to kiss his neck.

"Did Peja send you back to make nice?" asked Misha, softly.

"Yes, but that's not why I'm back."

"Show me why you're back."

Vera ran her hands down the front of his chest and reached for the top button of his Levis 501s. She started to slowly unbutton all the clasps, one at a time. Then she thrust her hand into his crotch and nipped at his ear.

"Can she give you what I give you?"

Misha groaned as he threw his head back.

Vera's tongue slithered down his neck as she continued to whisper in his ear. "She'll never understand where you come from."

She continued to stroke him from behind.

"She will never understand how they executed your grandfather and set his body afloat in the Sava."

Misha moaned.

"She will never know what it feels like to watch your mother die of sorrow and your father die of loneliness. I do."

She slowly and longingly kissed his neck as she quickened her pace with her hand.

Misha turned and said, "Oh, my Vera. *Sunce moje.*" My sunshine. "*Daj mi zivot.*" Give me life.

Vera lifted her skirt and straddled Misha, pulling his face to her breasts.

She rocked him and whispered in his ear, "*Ujedinjenje ili smrt, ljubavi moja.*" Union or death, my love.

Misha chose the obvious.

CHAPTER FIFTEEN
THE LONG ROAD TO CHINA

"As scarce as truth is, the supply has always been in excess of the demand."
Josh Billings

The Shanghai warehouse in Baoshan was five kilometers from the container yard and a world away from Miami. A dozen men worked non-stop to load the large containers with AK47s, 60mm mortars, various machine guns, shoulder-mounted rocket launchers which were to be used as infantry anti-tank weapons, and the "Red Parakeet" surface-to-air missiles. The facility occupied a site approximately 20,000 m² and had about 7,000 m² of warehouse floor space. Most days it was empty, but this last week the all-weather raised-floor bay was stocked to the gills with artillery. On the outside of the hangar, a sign read Shanghai Shipping Company.

Armed guards patrolled the perimeter of the warehouse and provided round-the-clock protection from would-be infiltrators. The arms smuggling business in China was lethal, run only by a handful of highly placed government officials with close ties to the Red Mafia. Their organization was foolproof. As a offshoot of the Chinese military, Shanghai Shipping Company thrived internationally with business lines including port terminals and warehousing, insurance, real estate and hotel management.

Li Chao, Shanghai Shipping's Group President and Chief Executive Officer, repeatedly denied any connection with the Chinese military and said, "We're only interested in making money." He insisted that the People's Liberation Army had no influence on the company's operations or global business strategy, and that Shanghai Shipping was a legitimate international conglomerate with close ties to international business leaders and the President of the United States.

The only sticky point was that the company's sole shareholder was the Chinese government.

Recently, Mr. Chao had signed an agreement with the Massachusetts Port Authority to begin a weekly shipping service between Shanghai and Boston, and expected to finalize negotiations to lease the Long Beach naval base in California soon. From Massachusetts to Washington D.C. to California, Shanghai shipping had greased enough political palms to make a dent in the coffers of a small nation.

The Long Beach Naval Station was tentatively placed on the *Military Base Closure-List* by the President in 1991. Critics screamed that the impact to Long Beach, California would result in 17,500 military and civilian jobs lost, and a direct blow to the fragile local economy with a loss of $52.5 million. Many also feared the closure would drive the California economy into the tank.

The Long Beach deal was due to be approved by the Secretary of the Navy who would turn over control of the Long Beach Naval Station, with a value of at least $65 million, free of charge to the city of Long Beach which had already agreed to lease it to the Shanghai Shipping Company of the People's Republic of China.

Mr. Chao had planned on leaving for the US at the end of the week to attend a huge black-tie gala on the *Queen Mary* in Long Beach, in celebration of the pending handover of the former naval base to the Chinese business delegation. Thanks in large part to Wilhelm Heidrich's lobbying efforts, Shanghai Shipping had secured a ten-year lease of the historic Long Beach Navy base and agreed to pay $14.5 million a year to lease the base.

To persuade China to take it off their hands, the city port promised to build a $200 million dock for container ships to bring Chinese goods into the United States. The Chinese would also have the option to expand the perimeter of the operation onto another 150 acres of old Navy shipyards that would be developed at the City of Long Beach taxpayer's expense.

To add insult to injury, Chao's lobbyists had also reached a firm "understanding" with Customs Officials that only two percent of the shipments would be inspected, leaving plenty of room to act with impunity.

Established in the name of economic redevelopment, the arrangement was considered an incredible business maneuver by the US Administration, and a betrayal of national security by others.

Opponents of the deal accused the Chinese government of establishing Shanghai Shipping for the legitimate use of its navy ships for civilian shipping, and a legal cover for the Chinese navy's smuggling. In 1985, the Chinese Navy had been linked to illegal smuggling of cars, TVs and other electronic equipment out of Hainan Island in the South China Sea. But the company was cleared as the National Security Council told alarmed US senators that there was no credible evidence linking Shanghai Shipping to illegal activity, including arms smuggling.

The company was also suspected of active involvement in several controversies in addition to a Russian AK-47 gun-smuggling episode on the streets of Oakland, California.

In another shocking incident, one of the company's ships plowed into a crowded boardwalk in New Orleans, injuring 116 people.

In addition, Shanghai Shipping had been fined $400,000 for a violation of US shipping law in connection with its practices involving bribery of government officials in order to avoid paying US tariffs on its imports at United States ports of entry. Six of the company's ships had been detained by the Navy and Coast Guard for violating international safety regulations just in the last year, and the Coast Guard had placed the company on a target list of shippers to monitor and search.

Not a great track record by most measures. But Shanghai Shipping's tentacles penetrated the highest echelons of government as a result of generous contributions to many political war chests.

In the early morning hours of a late day in October, Chao stood impatiently watching as men continued to load the containers and place the sealing label readying the crate to be loaded on the truck outside. "Hurry up," he called to them. "At this rate a donkey would get the crates to the docks faster."

He stood smoking a cigarette, as a small old man rushed to his side and whispered in his ear. Chao quickly walked to the office at the far end of the hanger, and froze momentarily before bowing slightly to welcome the man seated in front of his desk.

"Welcome," he said. "I am honored and humbled by your visit."

"My dear and loyal friend," chimed in the tall, slim stately man as he rose and bowed in return. "It is I who is honored."

Chao gestured for tea and the old servant shuffled away. "Everything is on schedule," he said, after a beat. "The shipment leaves in a few hours."

"Excellent," replied his American colleague. "Our friend in Connecticut will be pleased."

Both men walked over to the large glass partition and looked at the warehouse below.

"You know, Chao, our president's reputation is being dragged through the courts and the lawyers' bills are mounting. We are currently confronted with a long-term battle," he continued in an affable way.

"Of course," Chao responded, pulling out a small black book from his jacket pocket and scribbling a note. "We are pleased to assist our dear friend. I'll have it all arranged."

"Your generosity will not be forgotten," his visitor replied.

"We are all very privileged to have a man like you at the US Consulate," said Chao, respectfully lowering his head.

"Oh, and one last thing, Chao. Our friend in Connecticut would like for the shipment to remain on route. No deviations. It must arrive by next week."

"Of course. As our ancestors used the trusted trail, so shall we. Goodbye, my friend," said Chao, bowing at the waist. His distinguished visitor left as quietly and quickly as he arrived.

Chao's servant entered with the tea and poured a cup of the steaming hot liquid. Chao settled in his chair with an air of self satisfaction. The Year of the Monkey was already proving to be a profitable one, thanks to his ingenious use of the ancient Silk Road for transport. The iron horse of modern transport replaced the camels and horses of the past, and the ancient trade road that connected Asia to the Persian Empire, was once again in operation. Caravans of trucks were hauling the shipment to the Indian border where officials were already alerted to approve quick passage.

No other overland route has ever been surrounded by as much intrigue as the age-old Silk Road. While its primary function originally had been to bring highly-prized silken threads and cloth from the Orient to Europe and North Africa, many other exotic goods had followed those same paths over the Himalayas through the centuries, including one weapon which forever changed the way war was waged.

Gunpowder, known as "Black Powder," traveled in the caravans of the ancient merchants and thoroughly changed the course of human history. From its venerable source in China, it traveled the danger-laden paths of silks and spices and with it, traveled the knowledge to both remake and destroy the world.

Heidrich and Chao had chosen the old Silk route, a historical path of danger and mystique, to carry this most controversial of prizes—Heidrich's bounty of weapons aimed for Bosnia.

Chao looked at his watch. Dawn was breaking, and in a few more hours, the shipment would begin its journey. As it had in the past, the trusted Silk Road would once again tie the East to the West, allowing the Chinese to reach their destination with its precious cargo of destruction.

CHAPTER SIXTEEN
DANCE OF ANGER

"Patriotism is the last refuge of a scoundrel."
Samuel Johnson

Aegis sat bare-chested on the bed, rubbing the fatigue from his eyes. The sun was setting over Biscayne Bay, and streams of the receding daystar flooded through the venetian blinds, illuminating his South Beach hotel room. He had accomplished much over the last two days. After arriving at Miami International Airport, he had rented a car and headed for Miami Beach, knowing full well that his intended targets would be found within the perimeter of the peninsula.

Heidrich had been specific. There were to be no screwups. He wanted them all dead—not wounded, not paralyzed, just dead. It had taken him under twenty-four hours after landing in Miami to find the wayward group of assassins. *What fools*, thought Aegis. The whole Black Hand gang roamed about Ocean Drive in plain sight, drinking in the bars at night and parading semi-nude on the beaches by day. So much for being cunning and strident warriors. They were like amateur playboys running around the decadent beaches chasing would-be models and drinking themselves silly. They may have as well have held out a sign that read "Here I am … come kill me."

Aegis was tall, trim and pale with a sliver of gray hair outlining the contours of his angled face and had spent ten years with the French Foreign Legion in mortal combat in such war-torn areas as Angola and Djibouti. His years of training had prepared him to reap the benefits of a life of murder-for-hire, and it paid well. Heidrich was just one of his elite list of clients.

Walking out onto the small balcony overlooking the Atlantic Ocean, he called room service for another pot of coffee, and a late edition of *The Miami Gazette*. There was no article in today's paper about the bombings. No new leads. It looked like his other target was laying low. How Alex had become involved in this gang of Serbian terrorists wasn't his concern. His mission was clear, to eliminate the threat regardless of gender.

Aegis reached for his binoculars and focused on the outdoor terrace of the News Café. Every evening, without fail, the tawdry group of terrorists gathered for coffee and strategizing. He zoomed in to see Peja and his boys roughhousing each other, and then he saw Vera walk in. She kissed her fellow comrades one at a time, then sat down at the large sidewalk table, throwing a file in front of Peja. He watched as the gang leader picked up the papers and then marched each of his homegrown assassins one by one to the nightclub next door.

Apparently, the disco was their favorite meeting spot. Aegis already planted a listening device in the club's back room, and tuned in to get the optimal reception. Although he spoke no Serbian, his high-tech translation device provided real-time transcription of the conversations. Aegis prepared himself for another evening of eavesdropping, hoping to secure all the information he needed to finish the job.

"Where's Misha?" asked Peja, his voice crackling over the transcription device. The electronic translator was already printing out the beginning of many pages of text.

"Probably with that bitch," replied Vera venomously. "He's betraying us. Look at the file."

Aegis heard chuckling in the background, then shuffling as Peja grumbled and moved to answer the knock at the door.

"Who's there?"

"Joe Camel."

"Spare me your attempts at American humor," responded Peja as he opened the door and let Misha in the smoke-filled room.

"Where have you been?"

"The Caribbean is lovely this time of year."

Peja shook his head in amusement as he lightly slapped the irreverent assassin across the face. "You're your father's son alright. It's that asshole gene that never skips a generation."

The men all laughed. They rose and greeted the prodigal son with kisses, pulled out a bottle of slivovitz, and began pouring out shot glasses. A Serbian melody was playing in the background as Misha gulped down the plum brandy, grabbed Vera by the arm, and pulled her into a tight embrace. She struggled as he swayed to the music, and the men sang.

Moja mala nema mane,
niko nema tako lepe dragane.

My little one doesn't have faults
Nowhere are there such pretty *Draganas* (a name).

Misha released Vera and bent over the table for another shot of *slivovitz* as he sang his baritone accompaniment.

Ma nema, nema, nema ona nikoga
Ona voli samo mene jednoga
      (i jos dva)

She has no one, no one, no one else
She loves only me
(and two others)

"*Kao mamino mleko!*" Like mother's milk! Misha declared, his arms wide open, his head flung back while the others formed a circle, their arms around each other and danced a quasi techno-style *kolo* which traditionally reflected a history of struggle for independence and resistance to occupations.

The men moved like warriors, their arms extended in mid-air, displaying a proud soldier-like dignity then shifted into a non-rhythmic thrashing as they gyrated to the ancient melody. For a culture that had spent almost its entire existence in either war or in subjugation, their improvisation released a pent-up chaotic energy that only resembled insanity.

Kad zagrli, kad poljubi
u ljubavi sva se ona izgubi.

When she hugs, when she kisses
In love she forgets everything.

The gang members' voices rose in unison as they sat down breathless, and raised their glasses, "*Ziveli!*"

Peja sat quietly in the corner of the room reading the file.

Aegis listened to the revelry, and shook his head. His transcription device was malfunctioning. There were too many voices overlapping to get a good reception. But it didn't matter, they were just a bunch of drunks singing out of tune. The important stuff would come later.

"*Dosta*," Vera yelled, irritated by the level of testosterone in the room. She had just about had enough.

Misha weaved towards her, trying to play a cat and mouse game behind the table and chairs. He ducked as she aimed closed-fisted punches at his face.

"So, were you with your whore all day?" screamed Vera as she scratched Misha face.

He recoiled and touched the bleeding wound. A trickle of blood oozed out of the fine yet deep cut on his cheek. His long fingers traced the opening, and he licked his fingers tasting the metallic flavor of his own blood.

Misha turned to strike at Vera but was stopped by Peja who twisted him around, and pinned his arm behind his back. He forced Misha to the ground, and placed his foot on the side of his bleeding face.

"You bring shame to our good name," Peja said as he applied pressure on the open wound.

"What does Article 24 of our Constitution state?" demanded Peja as he pulled out a 22-caliber pistol and aimed it at Misha's head.

The other members of the Black Hand, stared in fear and firmly recited in unison. "It shall be the duty of every member to recruit new members, but it shall be understood that every introducing member shall vouch with his own life for all those whom he introduces into the organization."

"Has our brother broken this rule?" continued Peja, as he cocked the pistol and placed the barrel between Misha's eyes.

The men stared in silence as Vera rose to speak.

"Peja, *ja te molim.*" I beg of you. "*Pusti ga.*" Let him go.

Peja stared at Vera as he pressed the pistol further into the bridge of his forehead. "Did you not accuse him of betrayal?" yelled Peja, demanding that Vera respond.

Peja pointed at the file. "You accuse our brother of sharing our secret identity with the enemy. You say the proof is in the documents you provided."

"Yes," Vera whispered as she stared into Misha's lightless eyes. She began to cry.

The file contained information about Alexandra Miletic, the Croat-Serb journalist at *The Miami Gazette,* and current recipient of Misha's affections. Vera determined she was more Croat-American than her Serbian half would ever be, and therefore, a threat to the organization. Not only was she a half-breed, but one with a powerful weapon at hand—she had the eyes and ears of the American public. Her ability to throw a wrench into their plans was formidable, and she needed to be stopped.

"Then you know that the punishment is death," proclaimed Peja.

"No!" she protested. *"Nemoj, on nije kriv!"* Don't, he's not guilty!

Peja slowly retreated and calmly sat down, his pistol still pointing at Misha's head. He continued with his interrogation. "Did you reveal your identity to the journalist?"

Misha rose, his eyes defiant. "No."

"And what does Article 30 of our Constitution say?" demanded Peja.

"On entering into the organization, every member must know that by joining the organization, he loses his own personality," Misha responded in an impassioned voice. "He must not expect any glory for himself, nor any personal benefit, material or moral. Consequently, the member who should dare to try to exploit the organization for his personal, or class, or party interests shall be punished by death."

"Very good. And, Article 31?"

"Whosoever has once entered into the organization can never, by any means, leave it, nor shall anyone have the authority to accept the resignation of a member," recited Misha as he pulled out a knife and lunged at Peja, knocking him to the floor.

As he straddled Peja, the knife at the older man's throat, Misha pronounced the Black Hand's oath of allegiance, tears streaming down his face.

"I, Misha, by entering into the organization "Unification or Death," do hereby swear by the Sun which shineth upon me, by the Earth which feedeth me, by God, by the blood of my forefathers, by my honor and by my life, that from this moment onward and until my death, I shall faithfully serve the task of this organization and that I shall, at all times, be prepared to bear for it any sacrifice. I further swear by God, by my honor and by my life, that I shall unconditionally carry into effect all its orders and commands. I further swear by my God, by my honor and by my life, that I shall keep within myself all the secrets of this organization and carry them with me into my grave. "

"Amen," said all the men in room as they fell to their knees, crossing themselves.

Misha removed the knife from Peja's throat, rose and opened his arms like a supplicant to God. "May God and my comrades in this organization be my judges if at any time I should wittingly fail or break this oath!" He knelt down sobbing and lowered his head, his arms falling back to his body.

The older man reached for Misha. "*Moj sin*," cried the man as he embraced his patriotic assassin. "My son, I believe you."

Vera wept with relief as the two men rose. When Misha came toward her and took her in his arms, she called him *duso moja*, my soul, and together they moved across the nightclub floor.

"You're lucky you're so beautiful," he said as he kissed her forehead.

Ma nema, nema, nema ona nikoga
Ona voli samo mene jednoga
(i jos dva)

She has no one, no one, no one else
She loves only me
(and two others)

All this time Aegis had listened with every anticipation that they would make his job easier by killing each other. Now, instead of a cry of death, he heard an "*Opah*" as the gang poured drinks and danced again, as though nothing had transpired.

These guys have a screw loose, thought Aegis, pouring himself another cup of coffee and continuing to read the rest of the transcript. As usual, his job was ninety-nine percent boredom and one percent adrenaline-pumping mayhem and, by the looks of things, he would have to wait a little while longer for the fun part.

Aegis yawned and settled in for the night, turning on the television and finally settling on CNN. *Just a couple more days*, he told himself. After all, he was a patient man, and good things come to those who wait.

CHAPTER SEVENTEEN
THE BRIDGE OF FATE

"The very concept of objective truth is fading out of the world. Lies will pass into history."
George Orwell

Alex sat at her desk, pretending to work but in actuality was alternating between looking at her computer screen and rearranging her top drawer. The day had been uneventful so far. She strolled in late that morning, uncharacteristically glowing yet distracted. Jose had frowned as he recognized that post-coital blush, but hadn't asked any questions since Jason was out of town in New York on assignment, and he knew better than to rock the boat.

Puttering between the water cooler and the editorial offices, Alex fixed her gaze on the phone that wouldn't ring. *Why hasn't he called me*, she wondered. Then again, she had just spent a sensual evening with a complete stranger. Maybe he didn't have her phone number.

She had trouble concentrating, and kept looking at the clock. Normally she didn't have enough hours in the day, but today the minute hand took forever to move. Alex spent time playing computer poker, checking her emails a thousand times, surfing the web and drinking about a gallon of coffee. She was wired.

A chill ran up her spine as the phone shocked her from her cyber distractions. Alex quickly reached for the receiver and knocked over the lukewarm coffee sitting on her desk.

"Shit," mumbled Alex as she grabbed a napkin and blotted the spill.

"Alexandra Miletic," she answered breathlessly.

"Since when do you go by the name Alexandra?" It was Jason on the line.

"Oh, it's you."

"Boy, that's a warm reception."

"Sorry, Jason, I just spilled my coffee, and I'm working."

"Miss you too."

Alex told herself not to start with him. All this was not his fault.

"I tried calling you all last night," Jason lamented. "You didn't pick up."

"I know, I know," she soothed. "I was at my mother's and then I had a lead to follow up on."

"Well, it doesn't matter," he told her in a husky voice. "I'll be home in a couple of days and then we can pick up where we left off."

"Wow, I can't wait," she said, not bothering to hide her disinterest.

"What's wrong with you? You're being really weird."

"Nothing's wrong. I'm just tired. I didn't get much sleep last night."

"Can't get along without me, huh?"

"Listen, Jason, I'm working on a deadline. Can we talk later?"

"Jesus, Alex!" Jason said angrily. "Here I am putting my emotional self on the line and you're just blowing me away. What is up with you?"

"I'm sorry. It's not you. It's me."

"Well, that's always been the problem."

Alex didn't respond.

"I'm sorry," Jason said. "That was uncalled for."

"I really need to get going, okay?"

"Okay, honey. I'm sorry about what I just said. It's just that I hate being away from you. You understand, don't you?"

"Sure. I'll talk to you tonight," Alex replied dismissively.

"Love you, honey."

Alex hung up the phone.

She sat hyperventilating, suffocating in a shroud of guilt when Jose walked up to her desk.

"I'm buying," offered the seasoned editor as he took Alex by the arm. He led her to his office and pointed her in the direction of the leather couch in the corner by the window overlooking Biscayne Bay while he took a bottle of scotch and two glasses out of his desk's drawers.

He poured two stiff shots.

"Okay, *mi hija*," he said, a frown crinkling his forehead. "I'm no expert, but by the looks of you today you had one hell of a night last night," said Jose, as he stared at the dark circles under Alex's eyes. "My guess is that you weren't tap dancing with a bottle of scotch. At least not alone."

"Don't ask."

"Okay, I won't. But I hope it was worth it."

"You think I'm nuts, don't you," Alex asked him.

"Not nuts. No, that's not the adjective that comes to mind."

"Self-centered, bemused, irreverent, and possibly duplicitous?" she continued as she dazzled him with her ardent smile.

"You're getting closer. I'll settle for enigmatic."

Alex chuckled as she shot Jose a steamy glare.

"*Touché*," she said, winking at him. "You're the editor."

Alex stared out the window at the bay water glistening in the late day sunlight. Ripples of waves gently rocked the boats moored in their private docks, briefly straining the ropes that tied them to harbor.

"What was it like being a war correspondent?" she asked Jose out of the blue.

Jose raised an eyebrow then sat back on the couch and sighed.

"I mean, how did you stay objective when you were watching people die around you?"

"I don't think objectivity exists, *mi amor*. You do your best to report the facts as you know them, and hope that you've not been fooled by your own eyes."

"Was it that bad?"

"Yes," Jose told her, rubbing his grey beard. "There are only two kinds of people who go onto battlefields, soldiers and journalists."

He downed the last of his scotch. "I was so young when I went to Vietnam and was assigned to do a special piece on the men of Company B, 1/287th Infantry. They were stationed in the mountains and it was a month before the siege of a crucial valley below. What our boys didn't know back then was that a full North Vietnamese division was beginning to assemble to attack and keep us from the valley that summer.

"We were bombarded by the North Vietnamese that first day when we had to help evacuate the wounded. They suffered so many casualties. The rest, *mi hija*, is too terrible to remember. I wrote about it, but I don't want to relive it again. Death was too close. When those mortars started to fall your feet worked faster than your brain did. I was never an athlete, but let me tell you, I ran for my life. I was lucky. Many of those boys never came home. I cradled soldiers in my arms, knowing they would soon be dead. I felt the warmth of their intestines on my hand as I tried to press them back in … and the final gaze of a soldier about to die will stay with me forever."

Jose shivered. "The worst was when the napalm hit. It burned everything away and a gooey, white-plastic material dripped from the tops of the trees, still on fire. Men were engulfed by flames. I still hear their screams in my nightmares. We lost a bunch of our own men to the napalm and the North Vietnamese bunkers were destroyed. There wasn't a single North Vietnamese left alive."

Alex leaned over and gave him a huge hug.

"There's no glory in telling the tales of war, *mi hija*," said Jose, his eyes tearing. "The truth is always lost somewhere in purgatory."

"So, as a journalist, did you take sides?"

"I took the side of life," he said as he lifted his glass. "Here's to life, and to you, my dear."

He stared at Alex, his eyes narrowing. "Why are you asking me about this?"

"Just curious."

"That's bullshit. I know you better than that," he retorted as he walked over to his desk and shuffled through the pile of papers threatening to spill onto the floor.

"I think I'm getting too involved in this story."

Jose sat down behind his desk and put on his editor's hat. "And, how's that?" He reached for a half-smoked cigarillo sitting in the tiny ashtray and lit it.

"I can't get into all the details now, but let me put it this way. Watergate was nothing in comparison."

Jose laughed heartily. "Forever the drama queen, *mi bonita*. Obviously, I've given you too much booze."

Alex rose, hurt and confused, and headed for the door. "You were the last person I thought would knock me down."

"Wow! Wait a minute," said Jose as he grabbed her and ushered her into the chair. "I'm not knocking anything, but you come into my office, let me spill my guts about my time in Vietnam then wallop me with some wild statement about toppling our government."

"I didn't say that what I had would topple any government. What I said was … oh, never mind." Alex shrugged him off.

"Let's start over, *mi amor*," he said, trying to appease her. "What's going on?"

Alex stiffened in the chair. "I think you'd better sit down for this."

"The stage is all yours," said Jose as sat in his leather executive chair and puffed on his cigarillo.

"I have two very credible sources and some evidence that implicates very powerful people in an international arms smuggling operation," said Alex, her eyes on fire. "And that's not the worst of it. Apparently, these guys are former Nazis whom the government brought to this country through some dubious channels. It looks like the government sold its soul to the devil and continues to do so," said Alex, talking a million miles a minute now that she had started.

Jose's eyes widened, but he sat silent.

"And, to top it all off, these guys are now getting bumped off one by one by a ring of Serbian assassins in retribution for the killings committed in Yugoslavia during WWII, and because of their current involvement in shipping weaponry to the Muslims in Bosnia," she concluded.

Jose inhaled deeply. "So, what you're telling me is that your story not only has former Nazis on US soil running an arms smuggling enterprise that our government knows about, but you also have some rogue terrorist organization killing these guys off as some part of some personal vendetta."

"That pretty much says it all."

"And to think I kept you covering city council meetings all these years."

"Yeah, I almost didn't believe it myself until I read the file. I have evidence, Jose. Secret government documents that are not available through the Freedom of Information Act."

"How did you get your hands on them?"

Alex smiled. "I can't reveal my source, but let me put it this way. He's well placed in the FBI."

"And the terrorists? Do you have evidence implicating this gang?"

"You could say that. I have a source in the organization that's been feeding me information and will continue to do so."

"So, how does a nice girl like you get involved with an assassin?" asked Jose. Then his eyes widened in disbelief. "Never mind, Alex. I get the picture."

"No, it's not what you think!" she protested, her voice rising. "My source is not involved in the killing. He wants to bring them to justice."

"What role does he play then?"

"I'm not quite sure, but he's not a murderer. He can't be," said Alex, softly. "There has to be another killer out there."

"Watch your step," said Jose slowly. "The path you're taking is dangerous, and by the sound of it, you're already tripping over your own feet."

"I need you to back me up on this. I think I know who's in charge of the arms smuggling cartel. You won't believe me when I tell you."

Jose listened as she ran him through all the evidence. He asked few questions and at the end, sat dumbfounded and silent.

"I don't know, *mi hija*. This sounds too dangerous. Maybe I should get the brass involved," Jose said, picking up the phone.

"This is my story, Jose," she insisted, rising. "Give me a chance to bring in all the facts, then and only then, I'll hand over everything to the paper. But for the moment, there are a few too many holes that need to be filled."

Jose reluctantly agreed and put the receiver down. "Okay. I'll give you the time you need but I think you have bitten off more than you can chew."

"I know," she told him, her eyes worried. "But, I don't have much of a choice. I need to see this through."

CHAPTER EIGHTEEN
THE FLAMING SWORD

"We have just enough religion to make us hate, but not enough to make us love one another."
Jonathan Swift

Large palm trees swayed by the saltwater bay as Alex headed to her car in the employee parking lot. She quickened her step as the breeze picked up, dusting her face with a sprinkling of moist ocean air. Another storm heading northwest up from the Caribbean was due to hit the South Florida coast by morning, promising a deluge of rain. Alex got into her car and quickly locked the door. She knew she needed to be careful. For the last few days, she had felt as though someone was lurking, watching her from the sinister shadows.

Alex shivered as a cold chill produced goosebumps on her arms, as though the devil were walking over her grave. Feeling panicky, she peeled out of the parking lot and onto Biscayne Boulevard to head East across the causeway. She gunned the accelerator when she heard the chime of the alarm bell and saw the lights flashing on the drawbridge, and made it across just as the wooden barriers came down to stop the traffic.

Looking in her rearview mirror, Alex saw Miami's skyline coming to life as night fell, the buildings glowing a brilliant blue, red, green and gold to paint a deceptively vibrant picture of a city which was actually full of racial tension and poverty. Just a few blocks southwest of the *Miami Gazette* building was the ghetto.

But Miami was changing. A lot of money was being pumped into the city. Real estate tycoons and would-be magnates were investing millions of dollars to buy up and restore old yet architecturally unique art deco buildings. But the poor were being squeezed out of their neighborhoods as rents skyrocketed and the value of the land quadrupled overnight. Economic redevelopment was the favorite buzzword of politicians and business leaders alike. The only constant in Miami was change, but was it change for the better? Alex had her doubts.

Not feeling like heading home, she steered her convertible Mustang towards Lincoln Road and a quaint Argentinian restaurant on the far side of the long pedestrian walkway. She pulled her car into an empty parking spot on the edge of Alton Road and decided to walk. She needed some air.

Lincoln Road was gaining in popularity as many restaurants, art galleries, small local performance arts theatres and boutiques promised to revive the once decrepit and forgotten promenade. The street was full of expensively dressed patrons from Miami Beach and the occasional tourist hoping to discover a gastronomic jewel on the outskirts of the South Beach. But the sky was ominous and many were already headed indoors. Alex took a shortcut through the alleyway.

A blinding streak of lightening filled the sky and illuminated the back street as Alex picked up her pace. The bang of thunder followed a few seconds later—one one-thousand, two one-thousand, three one-thousand, four one-thousand, five one-thousand, and boom! The storm was about one mile away.

She ducked under an awning as the sky opened up, and it began to pour but, since she was only half a block away, Alex decided to make a run for it.

From a hidden entry, Misha watched as the sky suddenly opened and Alex ran into the restaurant, and just in time. Someone was tailing the journalist and aiming a semi-automatic pistol, equipped with a silencer. Misha carefully aimed and fired a muffled shot as another bolt of lightening cascaded across the horizon. An expert marksman, he hit his target without fail.

The shrouded figure slowly lowered the gun and sat on the wet ground, much like a rag doll. The gun dropped out of the assassin's hand as the puddle of rain water turned red. Misha stepped out, gun in hand, and walked to the slumped body. He noticed that the killer was still breathing. Quickly he turned the body over and removed the baseball cap, recoiling in horror as a mound of thick black hair fell from under the hood. Vera sat staring at him, a trickle of blood oozing out of her mouth. He dropped to his knees and took her into his arms.

"*Srce moje*," he cried as he stripped off the hooded sweat shirt and looked at her wound. It was fatal, the thick, red blood streamed out of her body as she gulped for her final breaths of air. Her lips moved, but no words came out. A tear gathered in the corner of her eye and slowly slid down her cheek. Smiling at Misha, she closed her eyes and fell into an eternal sleep, vanishing from his life.

Misha sat rocking her like a baby, his whole body shaking, as the rain pelted down on him.

"*Zasto*? Why?" he screamed as he folded her limp body in his arms. "I had everything under control. Why did you make me do this? *Moja* Vera. My Vera. My dear sweet, foolish Vera."

Knowing that he didn't have much time before someone discovered them. Misha quickly wrapped her up in his arms and ran to his car around the corner. Flipping the trunk open, he placed her body inside.

"Please forgive me," he said. It was almost a whisper.

He then drove towards Key Biscayne. There was only one spot close enough where he could get rid of the body.

Misha drove like a bat out of hell until he reached the Miami Seaquarium where he opened the trunk and pulled out a rope, a knife and Vera's lifeless body. The only way he could get in was by scaling the twenty-foot concrete wall, and he estimated that the antiquated surveillance system would give him just under a minute before the cameras rotated back to the south side of the entrance. Tying the rope around Vera's waist, he took the other end with him as he climbed the big pine tree next to the entrance, and then hurled himself at the wall, landing like an agile cat on a windowsill. Adrenaline pumped in his veins, and his heartbeat pounded in his head. He had under thirty seconds to get in and take cover. Hand over hand, he pulled at the rope and dragged Vera's bleeding body to the top. Grabbing her in his arms, he hurled her corpse into the bushes below and dove for cover just as the camera panned the area.

The seaquarium was silent except for the violent wind blowing the tree branches against the wall. Misha looked at the sky. The downpour was due to hit any minute as the storm headed southwest.

He threw Vera's limp body over his right shoulder and ran for the shark channel about hundred yards away. Placing her down gently, he quickly stripped her naked then whispered a prayer.

"*Oprosti mi, ljubavi moja*." Forgive me my love, Misha said as he crossed himself, his voice the barest croak.

He stood for a moment, holding her nude body in his arms and looking down into the shark-infested pool below. A few drops of blood had already fallen into the channel, and the sharks had begun to thrash in anticipation.

Misha dropped her body in and watched in horror as it floated on top of the water facedown. Why weren't they attacking? Sharks weren't domesticated. They were killing machines just looking for their next meal. Maybe he had made a mistake. He panicked as he tried to figure out how to get her body out of the channel. Suddenly, there was a violent splashing as the corpse was yanked under, legs first. Within seconds, Vera's body disappeared into the murky dark pool below.

Misha exhaled in relief as he picked up her bloodstained clothing. He stood listening to the fierce splashing for a few more seconds and then to the silence. The deed was done. Finally, he heard nothing but the incessant ringing in his ears and the soft whistling of his own breath. Within minutes he was headed back to South Beach. The night had just begun.

Alex checked out the menu and decided on a rare filet mignon, a baked potato, a green salad and a bottle of red wine. She sat looking out the window as the rain fell and the wind howled. Alex stared in disbelief when the waiter showed her the wine label before uncorking the fine vintage.

"I'm sorry," she told him in a flat voice. "I didn't order this Rothschild."

"I know, *señorita*, but the man at the bar did," replied the waiter pointing across the room.

"Oh Lord, not this again," muttered Alex under her breath and turned to see Misha smiling at her.

Her heart skipped a beat as she watched him walk over to her table and reach for her hand. He bent down and longingly kissed her palm, playfully running his tongue between her fingers.

"Shall I get you another glass," asked the waiter as he watched them undress themselves with their eyes.

"Yes, that would be lovely," responded Alex softly.

Misha sat in the chair beside her and placed his hand on her shaking thigh. He slid his hand under her skirt and slowly caressed her exposed skin.

"Have you ordered?"

Alex couldn't find her voice for a moment and nodded instead.

"Yes," said Alex finally after clearing her throat. "They have the best meat in town."

The waiter returned with another glass and her filet mignon. He poured the wine then quickly left as Alex whispered "thank you."

When she was served, Misha took the knife from her and offered her a slice of the rare meat before cutting himself another. In spite of herself, Alex became aroused as she watched him catch the juice with his tongue.

Alex felt guilty as her arousal mounted. She needed to break his spell.

"I don't even know your name," she said in a strained voice.

"My name is Misha."

"Well, Mr. Mystery Man Misha whatever your last name is, I'd like some answers if you don't mind."

"That's fair. I can't just expect to take you to bed again without a sharing of confidences."

"You're being rather presumptuous," retorted Alex, batting her eyes in feigned anger.

"No, I'm being honest, *duso moja*. You know it, and I know it. There's no avoiding that which God has already laid out."

"And what does He have in mind for us?" Alex asked, smiling sheepishly.

"You don't believe, do you?"

"What? Believe in God?"

"Yes."

"I don't know what I believe in. There are too many horrible things that happen in the world to believe that some loving deity is up there watching and doing nothing to stop it."

"Maybe he has empowered his sons and daughters to act for themselves in His name."

"Is that what you think?"

"I know that the path of the righteous warrior is paved with many blessings. And, I think that you're one of those blessings."

Alex melted as she stared into his intense dark eyes. How could she respond to something like that? He had the soul of a poet and the noble heart of a fierce warrior. Any way you looked at it, Alex was in for big trouble.

"When's your brawny American frat boy coming home," Misha asked, hostility in his voice.

"Who, Jason?" Alex was shocked. "How do you know about him?"

Misha smiled.

"So, you were the voyeur on my balcony that night," exclaimed Alex, her eyes widening with fury.

"*Nemoj da se ljutis*," Misha laughed. Don't be angry.

"Bullshit!" yelled Alex, her lower lip trembling. "Who the hell do you think you are?"

"Your guardian angel," Misha replied, not skipping a beat.

"I think I've just about had enough. I don't need you to protect me from anything," said Alex and she rose to leave.

"Once again you jump to conclusions before getting the whole story," Misha said calmly. "I would think that's a dangerous trait for a journalist."

"What the hell are you talking about?"

"I followed you to your apartment that night and saw someone waiting for you. I had to make sure that you were all right. Nothing more and nothing less."

"And, I'm supposed to buy that?" hissed Alex, slightly shocked at his admission.

"Yes."

"There's no arguing with you is there?"

"I find it a waste of time. It's better to make love," said Misha as he pulled her so close to his body that she could barely breathe.

Her hand caressed his chest and stopped just over his heart. "And the tattoo? What does that represent?"

"Drunken, adolescent foolishness."

"I don't believe you," replied Alex as she freed herself from his grip.

"If I told you the truth, I'd have to kill you," said Misha, almost smugly.

"Very funny."

Suddenly, an eerie silence filled the conversational void. Misha's piercing eyes met hers, and for a moment Alex felt as though she were looking the Devil in the face.

Alex was suddenly afraid. "What do you want?"

"Alexandra. I won't hurt you. But you need to know that you're in danger. We both are. Heidrich's sent someone to kill us."

She laughed nervously. "You're serious, aren't you."

Misha nodded. "We need to act quickly. I'll protect while you're in the process gathering all the information. You need to finish the story and expose this bastard."

"So, you lured me into bed, expecting me to do your bidding afterwards?" Alex asked, horrified by her realization.

"Why do you see things in such simplistic fashion?" Misha asked her. "Making love and making war are two separate things. One doesn't have anything to do with the other. I made love to you because I wanted to, and I still do. But this is bigger than the both of us. That bastard is out there and he's gunning for us. We either work together on this or we'll probably die our own separate deaths. You choose."

"So, I guess you weren't kidding when you said you were my guardian angel."

"I'm afraid not," said Misha. "Do your job, Alexandra. Print the truth, and I'll watch your back."

Alex took a deep breath as he leaned over and whispered, "Trust me."

Her gaze drifted sightless past him as she stared through the window at the flooded street. She was really starting to worry now. This was the second time this week that someone had murmured those same two words, asking her to make a leap of faith. Alex slumped back into her seat and poured herself another glass of wine, then ordered a second bottle.

CHAPTER NINETEEN
OF ARMS AND MEN

All wars are racist wars fought against the evil them by the self-righteous us.
David Roberts

A sky-blue flag with a golden sun and a steppe eagle in the center flew above the remote outpost as the caravan approach the Chinese-Kazakhstan border, the first of many crossing. The road rose steadily up a steep river valley that had once constituted one of the main routes on the old Silk Road. The border did not appear to be heavily defended.

A lone Kazakh soldier lifted his head, extinguished his cigarette and put his novel down as the trucks drove up the unpaved road and rumbled to a slow stop about fifty yards away. The border guard slowly laced up his boots and picked up his Kalashnikov rifle, squinting as he stared into the mid-day sun above the mountains. In the distance, there was another soldier on horseback, with an AK-47 strapped on his back, towing a spare horse behind him, slowly climbing to the edge of the ridge. He turned and looked over his shoulder, briefly stopping in mid-stride then proceeded riding over the hill, the sun at his back.

The two Kazakh soldiers were no match for the smugglers. The trucks were each equipped with a driver and three heavily-armed guards who sat ready with machine guns and rocket launchers.

When the USSR collapsed in 1991, Kazakhstan had declared itself an independent republic and was officially recognized by China within a month. At the beginning of the 1990s, the interconnectedness between China and

Kazakhstan had increased when air, rail, road and telephone lines linked Almaty, Kazakhstan with Urumchi, the capital of Xinjiang. Prior to 1992, cross-border trade was extremely limited between Kazakstani and Chinese border regions, but that was changing quickly as the route became a major thoroughfare for drugs and arms smuggling.

The Russian-trained officer was the first and most likely only line of defense against trafficking across Kazakh territory, and, with a salary equivalent to less than twenty dollars a month, the soldier barely hesitated in giving a green light and allowing the traffickers into the impoverished country on their way west to the Caspian sea. Anyone with a mule, a truck or a helicopter was whisked through for a hundred dollars and a ounce of heroin.

Chao's people in Xinjiang had already arranged for safe passage on both sides of the border. As the trucks left China, they passed by a small army post, manned by a squad engaged in digging holes and painting rocks. They barely lifted their heads as the officer in charge waved the caravan through.

There was no means of communication across the border between the Chinese and Kazakh guards except flag-waving. When the flags were waved, it alerted the other side of the checkpoint to be on the lookout. That afternoon there was only the gentle fall wind whipping the flag about in an indolent fashion, catching the frayed ends of the nationalistic red and yellow fabric and tossing it playfully in the air.

The Kazakh soldier watched his Chinese counterparts as they milled about a vegetable garden, cleaned their weapons, or relaxed bare-chested, soaking in the sun's rays. He put his rifle down as the trucks approached, waving and smiling as he ushered them through. The caravan left a cloud of dust behind as it continued on the desolate road, passing a plowed strip in front of double-lined barbed wire fencing surrounding the empty prison-style watchtowers.

The caravan continued along the bumpy road as the smugglers settled in for the long haul across the difficult terrain. They had two days to reach the Caspian Sea where a freighter, bound for the Republic of Georgia, awaited the cargo.

It was important that the smugglers keep on schedule since, once the shipment reached Georgia, another caravan of trucks waited to transport the arms-laden cargo across the mountainous terrain to a ship waiting to cross the Black Sea, and proceed through the narrow Straits of Bosphorus into the Sea of Marmara. They knew they had to land on Turkish soil by the beginning of next week, and by the looks of things, timing was tight. There was no room for error.

CHAPTER TWENTY
SHADOWS OF OUR ANCESTORS

"A lie told often enough becomes truth."
Lenin

Alex woke up as a torrential tropical storm howled outside. She had had trouble getting to sleep that night, and when she finally had, she had dreamt of the killer stalking her. Despite all the testosterone-driven bravado on the parts of both Misha and Agent Sommett, Alex realized she was alone against the faceless assassin.

She hugged the pillow tightly with one arm and stared at the ceiling. The rite of passage lay ahead of her and all she needed to do was intrepidly forge ahead. Her destiny was under her control. No one was going to dictate to her any longer. Not Misha, not Agent Sommett, not Jose, not Jason and certainly not the killer. She rallied to her bare feet and paced around the room reviewing the chain of events.

At dinner she had told Misha that their liaison was going to be a professional one from now on, and agreed that the story was bigger than the both of them. The drama of unrequited love was the last thing they needed. Misha had shrugged off Alex's new rule, but had promised to protect her before exiting without even a second glance.

After leaving the restaurant on Lincoln Road, she had gone home and called Jose. Alex knew she needed backup. If there really was a contract killer out there, she had to put all the evidence in a safe place, and she and Jose had agreed to store the documents in his office safe. They argued about the paper hiring a bodyguard for Alex, and Jose finally acquiesced and backed off as she insisted that her source provided the only protection she needed. At least for the time being.

Now, although she had a stack of mail to open and phone calls to return, Alex just sat staring at the pile on her desk. She needed to confront Heidrich with the evidence and soon. Misha was right. Heidrich was the mastermind behind the whole arms smuggling operation, but she needed not only to expose him, but also to protect him from this gang of nationalistic lunatics who were responsible for the bombings. She had to do something to prevent another cold-blooded killing even though the intended target was responsible for the deaths of thousands. Alex had to abide by the laws of justice and the workings of her own conscience. It was time for her to play at Misha's game.

She picked up the phone and called Jose.

"*Buenas dias, mi bonita.* I'm happy to hear from you," he said in a raspy voice.

"Did I wake you?"

"Hardly. I haven't been to bed," answered Jose. "I was up all night doing some research and I've come up with a way for you to get to Heidrich next week."

"I'm all ears," Alex told him, jumping out of her chair.

"It appears there's a huge black-tie affair in Long Beach, California next week," Jose continued. "Heidrich will be there along with a bunch of dignitaries. I can get you your press credentials and set up an interview through his PR person. We need to get something on the record from him."

"Brilliant!" exclaimed Alex. "You're the best."

"Listen, I'm not finished. It appears that this gala is rather controversial. There are a lot of people very upset that the naval base is going to be leased to the Chinese. Apparently, Heidrich really pushed the deal through and the White House has personally gotten involved, secretly lobbying the Navy and the City of Long Beach to go along with it."

"Interesting," said Alex. "So, Heidrich's also in bed with the Chinese."

"Seems like it. The Chinese deal is going forward without a national security review by either the CIA or the National Security Council. The White House has apparently avoided normal and routine government channels in pushing the agreement through."

"This guy has really wove a wicked little web of corruption, hasn't he," remarked Alex.

"I'll keep checking into this some more. But, for the time being, you have the go-ahead to go to California."

"I'm packing my bags."

Zvona was in the backyard removing the large palm fronds that had fallen onto the patio during the storm. A few strands of blond hair blew away from her stylish chignon as she bent over and swept the wet leaves. Coming up quietly behind her mother, Alex lightly smacked the older woman's bottom.

"Jesus, you scared me," cried Zvona as she pressed one hand to her heart. "I'm getting too old for you to sneak up on me like that. What are you doing here?"

"I missed you," said Alex, giving her mother a big kiss.

"Hmmm, that's suspicious. You must not have any food in the house."

"Come on, Mom. I don't just come over so you can feed me."

"So, are you here for some motherly advice?"

"What do you have in the fridge?" asked Alex as she went into the kitchen.

"And to think I almost believed you!" Zvona called after her, shaking her head in annoyance.

Alex sat at the white Formica kitchen counter munching on a piece of cold lamb she found in the refrigerator. "Do you have any milk, Mom?"

Zvona strolled into the kitchen, rolling her eyes at her spoiled daughter. "I'll check."

As Alex ate, she sat doodling Misha's tattoo on a paper napkin, deep in thought. She'd get over her disappointment. There was no room in her life for a man with a dubious background, let alone a man who had direct links to an organization of assassins. At that moment, Jason didn't seem so bad.

"Jesus, Mary and Joseph," cried Zvona as she stared down at Alex's amateur sketch. "Child, what are you doing?"

"I'm drawing," replied Alex, perplexed by her mother's outburst.

"I can see that. Where in the world did you see this?"

"I met someone with this tattoo the other day."

Zvona steadied herself against the table as she turned a pale white.

"Mom, what's wrong?" asked Alex as her stomach filled with panic. "Are you okay?"

"*Macane*," Zvona replied, lowering herself into a chair. "Do you have any idea what this tattoo represents?" she asked alarmingly.

"No, but obviously you do," Alex said, narrowing her eyes. "Mom, you have to tell me what you know." Alex anxiously sat in her chair as her mother began to recount the history of the Black Hand.

It seemed that on October 8, 1908, just two days after Austria annexed Bosnia, many men, including Serb ministers, officials and generals, held a meeting at City Hall in Belgrade where they founded a semi-secret society called *Narodna Odbrana* with the purpose to recruit and train partisans for a possible war between Serbia and Austria. The group also organized spies and saboteurs to operate within the Austro-Hungarian empire's provinces.

By 1909, the organization's work had been so effective that an outraged Austria pressured the Serbian government to put a stop to its anti-Austrian insurrection. As Russia was not ready to stand fully behind Serbia should things come to an ultimate showdown, Belgrade reluctantly complied and redirected the mission of the organization towards education and propaganda.

But, many existing members formed a new, clandestine organization to continue the terrorist actions. Ten men met on May 9, 1911 to form *Ujedinjenje ili Smrt,* Union or Death. This same group, also known as The Black Hand, embraced the professed goal to create a Greater Serbia, by use of violence, if necessary. Organized at the grassroots level in three to five-member cells to insure the secrecy of its members, with cell members only knowing their direct compatriots and its leader, the Black Hand trained guerrillas and saboteurs and arranged political murders.[9]

Alex sat transfixed as Zvona finished the rest of the history lesson.

In 1914, one of the group's leaders, Apis, decided that Archduke Franz Ferdinand, the heir-apparent of Austria, should be assassinated. Towards that end, three young Bosnian-Serbs were recruited and trained in bomb throwing and marksmanship. Three trained assassins were smuggled across the border into Bosnia via a chain of underground-railroad style contacts to execute the assassination. One of the members, Princip, succeeded in killing the Archduke on June 28, 1914.

The decision to kill Archduke Ferdinand was apparently initiated by Apis, although not sanctioned by the full Executive Committee, and the Black Hand probably realized that their plot would invite war between Austria and Serbia. In the end, however, there was no evidence that the Black Hand ever bargained on actions escalating into World War One.[100]

As the organization's tactics became more and more controversial against certain opponents and leaders who did not tow their party line, the government including Prime Minister Pasis decided to destroy the leaders of the Black Hand, once and for all dissolving the group. By the spring of 1917, many Black Hand leaders, including Apis, had been arrested.

A trial before a military tribunal was held in May of that year on charges that the Black Hand had attempted to murder Prince Regent Alexander. The charges included other counts of sedition and murder. Apis and five other men were sentenced to death. Of the five, two obtained commutations to long prison terms, but Apis and three comrades were executed by a firing squad on June 26, 1917.

By June 1917, the Black Hand was outlawed.

Alex couldn't believe her ears, but it was all falling into place. Apparently, Misha's group had revived the memory of the Black Hand and was continuing with its mandate—killing in the name of a Greater Serbia. This was the last missing piece of the perplexing puzzle. Alex now knew who she was dealing with, and the truth terrified her.

"So, will you please explain to me why in the world my daughter would meet someone who has a tattoo representing a terrorist organization that has been obsolete for over seventy years?" asked Zvona as she glared accusingly at her.

Alex opened her mouth to explain when the phone rang. Zvona got up to get the call. "Don't go anywhere. I want some answers from you," she called as she hurried to the other room.

Suddenly Alex's mother let out a scream. "No! God, no. We'll be right over."

"Teta Maria's in the hospital," Zvona explained as she reached for her purse and keys, with tears in her eyes. "She's had a heart attack and it doesn't look good."

Mother and daughter rushed out of the house and drove to Mount Sinai Hospital where they spent the afternoon talking with the doctors. Teta Maria was unconscious, her fragile heart furiously pumping for life. The prognosis was not good.

Zvona was inconsolable. Her older sister was the only immediate family they had in this country, and she was completely unprepared to lose her.

"If she dies, how are we going to get her back to Croatia to bury her?" cried her mother. "She would never accept being buried on foreign soil."

"Mom, don't talk that way. She's still alive!" exclaimed Alex.

"You know, she's been so distraught about this damned war. She's been holding small fundraisers at the church every week to raise money to send back. I knew it was too much, but she just wouldn't listen." Zvona broke down and sobbed.

"Mom, don't. We need to stay positive."

"What we need to do is pray," said Zvona, wiping her tears, pulling out her rosary beads. "Maybe God will spare her if we pray." Alex reached to hug her mother and rocked her as the older woman softly recited the Lord's prayer.

Oce nas,
koji jesi na nebesima,
sveti se ime Tvoje,
dodji kraljevstvo Tvoje,
budi volja Tvoja kako na nebu tako i na zemlji.
Kruh nas svagdanji daj nam danas
i otpusti nam duge nase,
kako i mi otpustamo duznicima nasim,
i ne uvedi nas u napast,
nego izbavi nas od zla,

Our Father, who art in heaven,
Hallowed be Thy name.
Thy kingdom come.
Thy will be done,
on earth as it is in heaven.
Give us this day
our daily bread;
and forgive us our trespasses,
as we forgive those who trespass against us;
and lead us not into temptation,
but deliver us from evil.

"Amen," said Alex. "We can't do any more sitting here. I think I should take you home."

Her mother reluctantly agreed, and decided to call Croatia to let the family know of Teta Maria's condition.

After dropping off Zvona, Alex headed home to a bottle of vodka. The loss of her dear *teta* was inconceivable. Ever since the disappearance of her father so many years ago, it had only been the three of them. They had braved conquering a new land, a new language and a new way of life, but they did it together. There wasn't a moment in Alex's life when Teta Maria hadn't been bustling about the house, cooking delectable Croatian dishes, singing folk songs and keeping the heart and soul of the family alive. Without her, Alex knew that theirs was a tenuous matriarchal web in danger of unravelling.

She sat down on the couch with the bottle and a glass, and lit a cigarette. God was testing her. More had occurred over the last two weeks than had ever happened in her twenty-seven years prior, and she wasn't prepared to deal with it. She started to cry uncontrollably.

Images danced before her eyes. She saw herself coming home from school to find her Teta Maria waiting with fresh baked bread, and a huge smile. She saw her at her high school graduation, beaming proudly and vigorously clapping, not understanding a word of Alex's valedictorian speech. She saw the sorrow in Teta Maria's eyes when she had finally moved out of the house to find her own apartment. That beautiful, round, cheerful pillar of strength had broken down and sobbed as Alex waved goodbye, leaving to begin a life on her own.

And finally, Alex watched as her Teta Maria slowly aged, her gray hair becoming more and more gray as the years past. She never expected that one day soon, she would lose her.

Alex quickly drank from the bottle, thirsty for comfort. Nothing else mattered. Not Misha, nor Heidrich, nor Jason nor the whole fucked up world. They could go and blow themselves to kingdom come! The only thing that mattered was that this beautiful, soulful woman was on the brink of death.

"It's not fair!" Alex cried, burying her face in her hands.

Suddenly she felt someone gently lifting her and holding her as she screamed at God. She tried to focus, but only saw a blurred face through her bloodshot, tearing eyes. She continued to cry and fell into the figure's arms.

"*Ja razumem.*" I understand, someone whispered.

Alex looked up to see Misha's face, his tears flowing, his eyes comprehending her deep sorrow.

"Get out," said Alex as she rebuffed his caresses. "You don't understand."

"But, I do, *malena.*"

"You're nothing but a liar and probably a killer for all I know."

"I'm neither."

"Have you no conscience?" screamed Alex, her eyes swimming in alcohol. "You don't have a monopoly on suffering!"

"Unfortunately, I don't," he said, trying to sound as reasonable as possible. "Let me help you."

Tearing herself away from him, Alex pulled out a desk drawer and waved a sharp envelope opener in front of his face.

"Okay, you bastard! Tell me lies!" She lunged, but her half-hearted aim was quickly thwarted as Misha easily wrestled the weapon out of her hand, and held her as she struggled.

"Alexandra, it's okay," he soothed.

"It's not okay. Nothing's okay," she whimpered. "Why her?"

"The most innocent souls are taken first and without mercy," he told her, holding her close against him. "Maybe it's because God already has a place waiting for them. He recognizes the righteous."

"But I'm not ready to let her go," Alex cried, a terrible despair in her voice.

"I know. I wasn't ready either when God took my mother. She, too, was an angel," explained Misha.

"She gave too much of herself while she was alive," he continued, turning to face Alex, his eyes shining sadly in the dim light. "The only thing that mattered was her family, and she watched as her father was dragged off to his death. She never recovered, and she then left me with my feeble father to try to cope with the loss. He wasn't capable of anything more than wallowing in his sorrows and finally ending his days. Alexandra, understand that I, too, am alone."

"Why did you lie to me?"

Her question was met with silence.

"That tattoo of yours, it represents the Black Hand. Did you honestly think I was that stupid?" she continued, trembling in earnest.

"I never took you for stupid. I was hoping it wouldn't matter."

"Oh, so I'm just supposed to sit back and say here's this guy who is part of some killer network from the past and I'm not to raise an eyebrow?" she shrilled. "You've got to be kidding me!"

"I won't let you kill him," Alex said, stressing each word.

"Then bring him before the world to judge," he replied, after a breath.

"I will. But beware, if you fall between the cracks of justice, you only have yourself to blame," Alex threatened. "I will not support your madness."

Alex rose from the couch and pointed at the door, "Now get out. I have work to do."

Misha left without a word as she wiped the tears on her cheeks, and picked up the file, determined to start writing the story of her life.

CHAPTER TWENTY-ONE
THE COLOR OF BLOOD

OLD TESTAMENT

Surely goodness and mercy shall follow me all the days of my life: And I will dwell in the house of the Lord forever.
Excerpt from Twenty-third Psalm

A sliver of a laconic moon rose over the Atlantic as Aegis sat on his hotel bed checking his ammunition, and cleaning his sub-machine gun. Based on the Black Hand's daily schedule, he knew they were due back at the nightclub within the hour, and he needed to be ready. Over the last two days, there was quite a bit of movement. The female gang member had already disappeared and Misha's attendance was sporadic. Aegis needed to act now before they all dispersed into some nebulous Slavic diaspora. He reached for his binoculars and walked onto the balcony, surveying the street below.

He watched as Peja and a couple of the other members followed one another into the club. They seemed nervous and irritable, looking behind their backs and yelling at each other. They were feeling the pressure, and that wasn't good.

Aegis went back into his hotel room and headed for the bathroom. He turned on the shower and grabbed his razor. *Cleanliness is next to godliness, or something like that*, thought Aegis as he climbed into the tub. His mother always told him that clean water would wash away all his sins. In his case, he wasn't sure that there was enough hot water in the boiler to absolve him of what he was about to do.

Once dressed, he packed his weapon and headed across the street. All hell was about to break loose.

The atmosphere was somber as the few members of the gang sat drinking and smoking, waiting for Peja to begin. Misha finally showed up, unshaven and dishevelled. His eyes were hollow as he sat down and declined a glass of slivovitz. He was obviously troubled.

"Where's Vera," asked Peja as he moved towards the men and pounded his fist on the table.

"I don't know," replied Misha. He continued smoking and looking off into the distance.

"*Ti lazes*!" yelled Peja as he grabbed Misha, accusing him of lying. "Where is she?"

Misha rose as the older man tightened the grip around his neck. Misha's face began to turn red. He swung at Peja's arm releasing the pressure and turned to face his leader.

"I asked you a question!" yelled the man.

"And I said I don't know. I haven't seen her for two days now. Maybe she found a new lover," Misha volunteered.

"That's not like her and you know it," said Peja as he lowered his voice and sat at the table. "I think someone's on to us."

The men all began to grumble.

"If they've already gotten Vera, then we're not far behind. We need to act now," said Peja as he shifted in his seat and sat forward. "We have the last three names, but we're only really concerned with Heidrich. By getting him, we cut off the head of the beast."

"So, why are we waiting?" demanded Dragan, a dark, heavyset gang member sitting at the far end of the table.

"There's been a slight change of plans. Misha and I are continuing on to California, and the rest of you are leaving for Bosnia. The fighting is picking up and our brothers need us," explained Peja. "The shipment is due to arrive in Dubrovnik some time next week and you need to head it off before the Muslims get it."

"But we don't know exactly where or when it will arrive," replied Dragan as he rose in protest. "We can't just show up in Dubrovnik and wait at the harbor like a bunch of wayward sailors!"

"I will have the name of the ship for you before it reaches land. You will confiscate the arms and then proceed to Bosnia and meet our brothers at the border," explained Peja, clearly annoyed at his underling's incessant demands for information. "Understood?"

"*Da,*" replied Dragan as he sat back down and sulked.

Peja was concerned. Since Vera's disappearance, the guys had become even more antsy, demanding many more answers to questions than they'd ever had before. He feared that he had the makings of a mutiny on his hands.

"And what about that Croatian journalist?" asked another member.

"What about her?" Misha demanded stiffly.

"Well, for one, are you done fucking her and two, if you are when are you getting rid of the bitch?"

"You insolent pig! " Misha shouted.

"Getting soft in your old age?" the man taunted him.

"I'll show you soft," said Misha as he threw himself across the table, and the two men fell to the floor, twisting as they rolled and threw punches.

Peja quickly rose, cocked his pistol and pointed the barrel at the two men. "That's enough!" he declared.

The men slowly parted, both shooting a menacing look in his direction.

"Misha. The end is coming and our brother is right. You need to finish her off," agreed Peja as he lowered the gun.

"She's interviewing Heidrich next week," Misha told him. "We'll get them both at the same time."

"Very good," Peja said. "The rest of you will have your plane tickets by the end of the day tomorrow. You leave the following day. Any questions?"

The men remained silent.

"A toast then," said Peja as he raised his glass in the air.

The men all rose and lifted their shotglasses of slivovitz. "*Za krst casni i slobodu zlatnu!*" In the name of the Holy Cross and golden freedom.

Just then, a figure stepped out from behind the bar and opened fire, sending a barrage of bullets across the room. Three of the Black Hand members instantly fell dead onto the table, their bodies almost sliced in half by the artillery fire. Two others, including Peja, lay wounded and bleeding on the floor, and in full line of fire. Misha and Dragan were the only ones not hit.

The two men zig-zagged across the room and dove for cover behind the large marble pillars, aiming their drawn weapons at the assassin. Dragan fired at the assailant as Misha lunged for Peja and dragged the man's wounded body behind an overturned table where they hunkered down as the killer opened fire yet again, spraying the room and killing the wounded men sprawled on the floor. The staccato of bullets ravaged their bodies, lifting their corpses off the ground as each bullet entered.

"*Idem od pozadi!*" yelled Misha to Dragan. He would take the back.

Dragan nodded and proceeded to empty his semi-automatic in the direction of the bar, buying Misha time to crawl under the curtain separating the two rooms.

Misha's heart raced as he circled around to the entrance of the club. He took a sharp turn and ran up the stairs to the second floor mezzanine, taking the steps two at a time. As he reached the landing, he aimed the gun over the balcony, quickly ducking as the killer emptied his round and ran through the back door. Misha stood up and looked below. Dragan was dead.

He doubled back down the stairs and ran to Peja.

"*Je si ziv?* Are you alive?" yelled Misha as shook the older man.

Peja rolled over holding his bleeding stomach. "The bullet went straight through. I'll be alright."

"Can you walk?"

"Yes, I think so."

"Let's go!" Misha reached under Peja's armpits and hoisted him off the floor, wrapping his arm around the wounded man's waist. "We don't have much time."

"What about the others?" asked Peja as he looked around the room and saw the rest of his men lying motionless.

"They're dead, and so will we both be if we don't get out of here now!"

The two men stumbled out of the back door of the night club. As they ran down the alleyway, they heard sirens in the distance, punctuating the still night air with their ominous wailing.

CHAPTER TWENTY-TWO
THE SEASONS OF LIFE

"Courage is the price that life exacts for granting peace."
Amelia Earhart

Teta Maria died at 2:00 AM that morning. When they reached the hospital, Alex and her mother found her at peace, her face serene, almost smiling as she lay in her bed, her hands crossed over her chest. Alex sat by the her aunt's bedside and caressed her face. She imagined a sweet angel sweeping into her hospital room, gently taking her *teta*'s hand and showing her the celestial road up to God.

Zvona had busied herself all morning with the food and drink for the wake. The small cast of Croatian mourners started arriving at the house at eleven, and milled about frenetically setting up the tables, and cooking in the kitchen. The church service was scheduled for that afternoon with the burial shortly thereafter. Alex was comforted by the presence of so many of her mother's friends who surrounded Zvona in this hour of need.

Jose had met Alex at the hospital and hadn't left her side since. He had also called Jason in New York, and he headed back on the first plane out of LaGuardia. They would both escort her to the church and then to the cemetery.

Alex dressed in the only black suit she owned, and headed to the small white church in North Miami Beach with Jose and Jason beside her. More than 150 people showed up, piling in shoulder to shoulder, to listen to the Catholic sermon and pay their respects to a woman who was very much loved for her generosity and unbridled spirit.

The day was clear and crisp and a gentle ocean breeze blew inland from the Atlantic. The sun streamed into the church through the multi-colored stained glass windows depicting biblical passages, and illuminated the congregation in a brilliant light.

After the sermon, they headed to a small cemetery in Miami where Teta Maria was laid to rest. Alex and her mother threw roses on top of the coffin as they lowered it into the ground.

Jason held Alex as she cried, her body shaking as she watched the first shovelful of dirt land on the coffin. Turning her tear-streaked face away, she stared at the pine trees lining the cemetery walls and saw a figure standing behind the trees, crossing himself. It was Misha. She watched as he lowered his head in respect, turned and walked through the cemetery gates, a slight limp in his gait.

Alex hadn't had much time to think about Heidrich and the business of war today, but Misha's presence brought her back to that unpleasant reality. She was due to leave for California tomorrow to once and for all confront this man who was responsible for so much misery. In some indirect way, she blamed him for Teta Maria's death. He and his kind were largely responsible for capitalizing on the misfortunes that had befallen the people of her native land. And, those who profit from the misery of others are as guilty as those who pull the triggers.

When the mourners started leaving the cemetery grounds for Zvona's house, Alex asked Jose and Jason to leave her alone for a moment to say goodbye.

"So, Teta Maria," said Alex aloud, bowing her head. "I guess this is goodbye. There are so many things I want to say to you, but I just can't seem to find the words. I hope you'll forgive me. I don't know why, but I don't feel like you're really gone. Tell me what to do. I'm so confused," Alex whispered as she put her head in her hands and sobbed. "Tell me how I'm supposed to find my compass in life without you!"

And then, Jason's arms were about her. As he led her to the car, she turned back to look at Teta Maria's grave and saw a black crow land beside the mound of dirt, piercing Alex with its gaze. It let out a sorrowful squawk as it picked at the earth then flew away.

"Watch over me, *teta*," whispered Alex as she got in the car, shivering as an ominous feeling of doom overshadowed her.

By the time they arrived at her mother's house, most of the mourners were already there, drinking wine and slivovitz and eating the Croatian delicacies proudly displayed on the large dining room table.

Zvona walked up to her daughter and held her tightly. "It was a beautiful ceremony, don't you think?" she asked, pride in her voice.

"Yes, Mom," agreed Alex, a weary sadness in her gaze. "I'm sure Teta Maria is smiling right now."

Her mother wiped a tear away before going back to the kitchen to direct her small army of cooks. Alex smiled. It was better for Zvona to occupy herself with the issues of food rather than sorrow.

Jose and Jason were busying themselves picking up the dirty plates and talking with the guests. What a couple of gems they were, thought Alex, shaking her head in gratitude as she walked up to the both of them and smiled. They were her true guardian angels.

"Thank you for being here," she said as she laid her hands on their shoulders.

Jason turned and looked at her with sorrowful eyes. "I'm sorry, Alex. She was such a lovely woman."

Alex nodded and gave him a big hug as Jose piped in. "Okay, you two. We need to keep up with the dirty plates." Jose grabbed Jason and pointed to the kitchen. "The baklava is ready. Let's stay with the program."

Jason obliged and walked away as Jose turned to Alex. "You know, you don't have to leave tomorrow," he said.

"Like hell! I'm going to get this bastard." Alex took Jose by the arm and led him to a small sitting room where she reached for her purse and pulled out the file and a diskette.

"Here you go. It's the whole dossier, and the article is already written except for Heidrich's comments, of course."

"We don't have to talk about this now," interjected Jose.

"It's okay, Jose. I'm fine. For some strange reason I feel really strong," Alex told him. "I think Teta Maria is looking over me." said Alex.

"Very well then," replied Jose as he reached into the top pocket of his double-breasted suit. "Here's your ticket and your hotel reservations. Go get him, *mi amor*."

Alex nodded then reached over and kissed his wrinkled cheek. "You'll take care of my mom while I'm gone?"

"*Si, mi hija.* Don't worry."

Alex patted his shoulder then headed to the kitchen. Jason was wearing one of her mother's aprons, and stood washing the pots and pans with his sleeves rolled up and soap suds up to his elbows.

"You're quite a sight," Alex joked as she came up behind him and wrapped her arms around his waist. He turned and playfully placed some soap bubbles on her nose.

"My mother didn't raise no slacker," he responded as he turned to finish the last of the coffee cups.

Alex grabbed the dishtowel and threw it in his direction. He wiped his hands and then took off the apron. "So, honey. Jose tells me you're leaving for California tomorrow. You should get some rest," he said as he unrolled his shirt sleeves. "I'll take you to the airport in the morning."

Alex nodded and they entered the living room and said goodbye to her mother and Jose.

As they walked in silence down the residential street towards Jason's car, he placed his arm firmly around Alex's waist. She rested her head on his shoulder. "I don't know what I would have done without you today," she said as she nuzzled into his warm body.

"You won't ever have to do without me, honey," he told her as he kissed her forehead. He looked into Alex's eyes. "You know how much I love you, don't you?"

"I'm the bane of your existence," responded Alex, her eyes glistening with tears.

"I wouldn't have it any other way, my love."

Suddenly they heard the rustling of the bougainvillea bushes across the street. Jason looked up and directed his gaze towards the noise, his forehead frowning under the street light. Then he shouted, "What the hell?"

A hooded man jumped out of the vegetation pointing a gun at them. Jason's eyes widened in horror. He pushed Alex over the small picket fence surrounding her mother's property, and dove for cover as a muffled shot rang out.

Alex's heart pounded as she crawled to look between the opening in the hedge and saw a man race across the street towards her. Jason was lying facedown on the sidewalk.

Alex crawled along the fence to a large rose bush and hid behind it, scratching her face against the sharp thorns. She watched as the man leaped over the hedge in pursuit, his gun searching for its target. Sitting in silence, barely breathing, she heard his footsteps slowly approaching her hiding place. *This is it*, thought Alex. There's no escaping. Frantically looking left and right, she realized she was trapped. She closed her eyes and mumbled some lame rendition of a passage from the Bible.

She opened her eyes to see the figure three feet from her and then saw someone jump out of the shadows and tackle the assailant, knocking him to the ground. Alex watched as the bodies rolled across the grass, listening as they landed punches on exposed skin. One of the men stood up and kicked the other in the stomach before racing off across the front lawn, high jumping the fence and running towards a black sedan parked at the end of the block.

Her savior lay moaning on the grass, momentarily tucked in a fetal position. Then he slowly rose and limped towards Alex. She watched as his face came into the light. It was Misha!

But first there was Jason's motionless body beyond the fence, sprawled on the sidewalk.

"No!" she yelled as she ran to his side.

Turning his body over, she checked for injury, her fingers warm with his blood were wet as she passed her hands over his right shoulder. Jason opened his eyes and moaned.

"Jason! Speak to me!" she cried, shaking him.

"Ouch, that hurts, Alex!" responded Jason as he reached for his wounded shoulder. "Jesus, what the hell is going on?"

"You'll be okay, honey," Alex told, breathless with relief. "You've been shot," explained Alex soothingly.

Jason tried to sit up and then, seeing the sight of his own blood on his shirt, fainted.

As Alex caught him in her arms, Misha rushed out from behind the bushes and grabbed her. "We need to get out of here!"

"Let go of me," protested Alex, shaking him off. "Jason's been shot. I can't leave him like this!"

Misha ripped open Jason's shirt and examined his shoulder. He shook his head, "It's only a flesh wound. He'll be fine. Besides, I can hear people coming from your mother's house. They must have heard the gunshots. They'll take care of him. Come on, Alex! It's now or never."

Alex looked at Jason. "Sorry, honey," she murmured. "But this has all got to stop once and for all."

Within seconds they had run down Pine Tree Drive to a car parked on the corner of 31st Street. Misha pushed Alex in the back seat then he got in on the passenger side. Another man was at the wheel. The car sped off.

At the same time, a white van parked at the end of the block roared its engine, and took off in pursuit. Inside were Agent Sommett and two other government agents, surrounded by high-tech equipment. They were on the radio communicating with base control.

"It's Legs! Jesus, they've got her," cried Sommett as he hit the agent behind the wheel. "Move!"

"Are the cameras rolling?" he asked.

"Been rolling, sir! Been rolling, report it!" replied the information specialist as he hit the "record" button.

A burst of static punctuated the interior of the van as Sommett radioed command. "Mike 15-7. Reporting "Flash One." Subject Lena Echo Gulf Sierra appears to have been abducted. Request instructions. Over."

"Routing, standby, sir … routing, standby," responded the voice over the radio.

He listened to the hum of the computer terminal as the radio transmission continued, "Confirm report, sir!"

Sommett stayed with his transmission as the van screeched onto 41st Street, following the black sedan back down Collins Avenue, towards South Beach. "Request instructions! This is happening now. We have one shooting victim and a kidnapping in progress. Flash status. This is for real!"

"Maintain position. Follow the principle. Transmit films encripted now. Do you copy?" said the voice over the radio.

"Roger," replied Sommett.

"Potomac out."

The van wove in and out of traffic following the sedan. As the agents turned onto Washington Boulevard, the driver sharply hit his brakes as the van skidded to a stop. The traffic was at a standstill as demonstrators gathered around the Holocaust Memorial, protesting the war in Yugoslavia.

"Damn!" yelled Sommett as he looked out the window and saw the sedan turn into an alleyway half way up the block. Jumping out of the back of the van, he ran down the street at full speed. Looking down the first alley to his right and seeing the car parked at the end of the back street near a stationery store, he drew his gun and slowly approached from behind only to find it empty. Misha, Alex and the third man were gone. Sommett hit the roof of the car, and stood panting. He had lost his target.

CHAPTER TWENTY-THREE
NOTHING TO DECLARE

"Hell hath no fury like a pacifist."
Solomon Short

The freighter passed through the complex, narrow waterway more akin to a river than a strait and headed into the hazardous and dangerous sea lane that connected the Black Sea to the Sea of Marmara. The captain was a savvy sailor and knew that the Strait of Istanbul ran approximately 16.74 nautical miles long, with an average width of 0.81 nautical miles, making for difficult navigation. The current was reaching seven to eight knots and the necessary course alteration was eighty degrees to keep the vessel on course.

Some thirty minutes prior to reaching the Turkeli Light House, the captain had contacted the Control Station by VHF Channel Thirteen and asked for permission to enter Bosphorus. He received the green light, then proceeded to advise his position and stood by until he entered the Bosphorus Straits, switching then to VHF Channel Twelve until leaving the Strait.

The captain messaged ahead in morse code for a pilot to assist in navigating through the Straits, minimizing the risk of accident. He knew that if he didn't accept, he would have to wait his turn at anchorage before entrance to the straits as the vessels with pilots had a greater chance to enter the strait upon arrival. He yelled at his sailors to prepare the pilot ladder for boarding.

His men met the pilot and welcomed him on board.

The Istanbul Bogazi or the Bosphorus Straits separated Europe and Asia, and the ship steamed through towards the Istanbul port. Passing under the

Bosphorus bridge, one of the world's largest suspension bridges with a vertical clearance of sixty-four meters, the captain stood in the control room looking at the city lights as he maneuvered his vessel.

Turkish officials awaited the arrival of the cargo ship at the harbor. They had been alerted that the shipment was to arrive some time that day and they already prepared the paperwork. A perfunctory walk-through was all that was necessary to rubber stamp the cargo, and they were working overtime.

The ship pulled into harbor at 12:15 AM and the Turkish customs officials boarded without delay. The Georgian captain presented his documentation and proceeded to show them the cargo in the hull of the freighter.

"As you see, we are transporting toys to Croatia," said the captain in Russian. The Turkish officials nodded, not understanding a word. They had already received their portion of the payoff and were oblivious to the contents. Whether the cargo contained Barbie Dolls or ground-to-air missiles, did not matter. They had to follow procedures and conducted the inspection in haste.

They verified their checklist. The country of the shipment's origin was China, and the exporter was Shanghai Shipping. The destination country was Yugoslavia, or the port of Dubrovnik. The value of the invoice was about twelve million deutschemarks, payable upon receipt. Everything seemed to be in order.

At the end of the inspection, the captain and the customs officials shook hands as the ship received the go-ahead to continue. The captain along with the Turkish pilot re-boarded and set for the Dardenelles Straits and the Aegean Sea.

By now, the winds were coming in from the south and were reaching gale force levels, accompanied by low cloud and rain. The captain was fully aware that the transient Mediterranean lows moving northeastward across the Aegean and Black Seas brought the most hazardous weather to Istanbul.

The ship's captain knew the timing was tight, and with any worsening of the weather conditions, they would miss their target due date. They had three days to reach Dubrovnik, and he prayed that the weather would cooperate. If not, heads were going to roll, starting with his.

CHAPTER TWENTY-FOUR
LITTLE HARD ONE

"A life lived in fear is a life half lived."
Spanish Proverb

Jason was still sleeping when Jose walked into his hospital room that evening. He was lucky. The bullet had just grazed his shoulder, causing a minimal amount of damage, but the way Jason was acting, you'd think he'd just come through major surgery. He opened his eyes and moaned as Jose took a seat next to his bed.

"So, son, how are you feeling?" asked the editor.

"I feel like I've been hit by a truck," Jason complained as he shifted in bed and slowly sat up.

"I know you're still a bit groggy," Jose told him, "but I need to know what happened. The police are outside waiting to speak with you, but before I let them in, I need to know where Alex is."

"Boy, I'm not sure," Jason said, resting his head on the propped pillow. "The whole thing is such a blur in my mind. It happened so fast. I didn't see him coming."

"Who?"

"Some guy was hiding in the bushes across the street and the next thing I know, he leaps out pointing a gun. So, my first reaction of course was to protect Alex. I threw her over the fence to get her out of the line of fire, and then I took a bullet as I was trying to shield her."

Jose took a deep breath and tried to remain calm. "Okay, son, we know all that," he said. "By the way, you'll be fine. The bullet only skinned your shoulder, and the doctors will be discharging you tomorrow morning."

"Man, this hurts," Jason complained as he placed his hand over the bandaged wound. "How many days can I take off for being shot?"

Jason wouldn't have done well in Vietnam or any other war zone, thought Jose, and then reminded himself to keep calm. After all, the boy was on drugs.

"What happened to Alex?"

"Well, the last thing I remember is that she was leaning over me, telling me I was bleeding like crazy and thanking me for saving her life and all, and then some guy comes over and rips my new Brooks Brothers shirt and I passed out," explained Jason. "Damn, that was a $70 dollar shirt!"

"Jason," the editor said in an exasperated voice. "Do you know where Alex is?"

"No, but I'd figured she should be here by my bedside. After all, I saved her pretty ass!" Jason said as his eyes rolled in his head. He was fried.

Jose thanked Jason for the information and huffed out of the room, walking up to the night attendant at the nurse's station.

"Excuse me, miss," he said to the young nurse. "I was wondering how my friend in room 204 was doing."

"Oh, you mean 'Mr. I-have-a-low-tolerance-for-pain, please-give-me-another-shot-of-morphine, Jason Parker?" replied the nurse, flashing a 100-volt smile.

"He's the one," sighed Jose as he smiled sheepishly.

"Yeah, he's pretty much done with medication for the evening. The doctor is releasing him in the morning, and if I had it my way, he'd be out tonight," she informed him. "Are you done with your visit because the cops want to question him," the nurse asked.

"Yes, thank you," replied Jose as the started to walk away down the hospital corridor, pausing to watch as the two police officers entered Jason's room and he heard the young man's voice echoing down the hallway.

"Gentlemen. Glad you're here. You know I'm lucky to be alive. If it wasn't for my martial arts training ..."

The door closed behind the officers as Jose smiled and muttered to himself, "Good luck, boys, you're going to need it."

Jumping in his car, he headed back to Zvona's house. This wasn't that poor woman's day. First she had buried her sister and now her daughter was missing. It was time for Jose to tell her the whole truth about the story Alex was working on.

He drove up as police investigators were still checking for clues on the front lawn of the house and Zvona ran out to greet him.

"Where is she?" she demanded, her eyes wide with panic. "Did Jason know what happened to her?"

Jose led her back into the house and they both sat down on the couch.

"We need to talk, Zvona."

"Oh, dear sweet Jesus!" she cried. "I can't take much more of this!"

"I think she's okay, but she's been working on this story and I'm afraid it's gotten rather ugly," explained Jose.

Zvona listened in horror as Jose told her about her daughter's investigation.

"This is unbelievable," she cried. "Why did you let her get involved in this mess!"

"I couldn't stop her," replied the editor, shaking his head. "She's no shrinking violet."

"So, what do we do?"

"It's out of our hands now. I've called Alex's contact at the FBI and he's on her trail. Don't worry. We'll get her back safe and sound."

Alex's mother was on the verge of tears as Jose reached over and took Zvona in his arms. "Don't worry, Zvona," he murmured, caressing her back. "I'll make sure she comes back to us if it's the last thing I do on this earth."

"Promise?"

"Promise."

Jose rose to leave as Zvona grabbed his hand and pleaded. "Don't go. Please. I can't be in this house all alone. Not now."

He stared deeply in her eyes, and her pain cut through him like a burning ember. His emotions bubbled to the surface for the first time in many years, and he took her in his arms. "I'm not going anywhere," he said as he led her to the bedroom. They dozed off, clinging to each other.

CHAPTER TWENTY-FIVE
THE TERROR NETWORK

"No revolutionary war can remain a purely internal affair."

David Galula

If trouble weren't her middle name, then Agent Sommett figured it should be. Damn that crazy girl! Now she'd gone off and gotten herself kidnapped, and the worst part was that it was on his watch. How could he explain to his superiors that their only source to the killers was missing in action?

His office was in an uproar. Yesterday, five dead bodies believed to be those of the phantom bombers had been found in a nightclub on South Beach. Whoever had killed them was now after Alex. The FBI had gathered evidence of her meetings with an unknown Serbian operative named "Misha," and they were planning to follow him and storm the terrorist compound later today, but something had gone terribly wrong. Someone had beaten them to the punch and slaughtered the whole lot of them in broad daylight. Sommett was troubled. There was yet another assassin out there, gunning for Alex and Misha, but why? Who was he?

The agent had at least five dead bodies on his hands, a journalist running amok with one of the terrorists and the Bloodstone file, and some mystery killer hot on their trail. If he didn't act quickly, Alex wasn't going to be alive for very long, and he'd have all hell to pay.

How he had allowed this operation to get so screwed up, he'd never know. His orders were specific. Two months ago, the Deputy Director himself had called Sommett ordering him to put his ongoing investigation of Bloodstone on the backburner. Sommett had been shocked. He had spent the better part of three years compiling all the evidence of Bloodstone's connection to illegal arms shipments to terrorist organizations around the world, and someone had put a stop to his inquiry. He had never known why, but he had his suspicions.

The world had changed. Enemies of old were now considered allies, and former allies now enemies of the state. The Bloodstone connection was playing a major role in supplying the Bosnian Muslims with much needed arms to fight the Serbs, and clearly the U.S. government didn't want to disturb the order of things.

The Balkans was a breeding ground for the return of terror, but terror with international implications. Although France, Britain and Russia initially had provided arms to Serbia, the United States along with Germany and Iran had been involved in covert airlifts of weapons into Croatia and Bosnia from the start of the conflict. And, the United States government, which had originally trained Afghan Arabs during the war in Afghanistan, supported these same Islamic fighters in Bosnia. The mujahadeen were financed by Saudi and United Arab Emirates money and received the financial and military support from Osama Bin Laden's network, all with the blessing of the United States.

What a mixed bag of characters, thought Sommett, but he understood all too well that the success of any terrorist organization was dependent upon the interests of an outside power, and every major superpower and lesser powers had their hands in the Balkan kitty.

But the delicate workings of international relations wasn't his department. There was one thing and one thing only that his government wanted him to do—to put a stop to the assassinations of the Bloodstone members, and at any cost.

His plan of action was perfect, but there was one problem. He had miscalculated Alex and her insane tenacity to dig for the truth. All she had to do was lead him to the terrorists, and he would take over from there. She would have had her story, and he would have gotten his promotion. But no, she had to keep digging and getting herself more and more involved in this international circus, and now she was missing.

Agent Sommett paced around his office as he tried to map out his next move. He needed to contain the situation, and fast. Then it dawned on him. Riffling through some papers, he found a five-day-old intelligence report. Heidrich was due in Long Beach this weekend for a gala on the *Queen Mary*. So that was it! The remaining gang members were going to assassinate the leader of Bloodstone, and in plain view of the public, to boot. He panicked. This was not what Washington had in mind.

The President of the United States was due to attend the party, along with many Senators and business leaders, and Sommett knew that Alex's bloodhound nose caught a scent of the intricate conspiracy and set her sights on exposing Heidrich. She was going to blow the lid off the whole operation! He needed to get to her first.

Intelligence reports were coming in fast, and Sommett grabbed the printout as it came over the line. His suspicions were confirmed. An Alexandra Miletic had boarded an American Airlines flight out of Miami bound for Los Angeles late last night and had landed at LAX three hours ago.

Sommett grabbed the phone and yelled, "Get me on the next flight to LA. This is urgent!"

CHAPTER TWENTY-SIX
WORLD WITHOUT END

There are only two mistakes one can make along the road to truth: not going all the way, and not starting.
Buddha

Alex woke up as the plane was approaching Los Angeles International Airport. She had spent a restless few hours crammed in between Misha and a Hollywood agent who wouldn't shut up. After six gruelling hours sitting next to this wired out wannabe, Alex was ready to sign anything he put before her. She expected he was great at his job.

"And she's the best. I have to tell you not only is she gorgeous but she's a beautiful person," continued the agent as he wiped his nose. Alex suspected he was doing coke in the bathroom, and the way she was feeling she wouldn't have minded a line herself.

"Talent and beauty. Now that's a combination. Okay, maybe she didn't come out of Julliard, but the girl has the best tits in town!" said the thirty-something Harvard dropout turned Hollywood lackey. "God, I love this business."

Alex couldn't stand another minute. She looked over at Misha who sat dozing peacefully and wondered if he was packing, then quickly put on her headphones and reflected on the last twenty-four hours. Alex was still a bit shell-shocked. Yesterday had been the worst day of her life. Teta Maria's funeral had been almost unbearable, and then Jason had been shot by Heidrich's contract killer. If it weren't for Misha, she'd probably be lying on a cold metal slab in the morgue right now. As much as she hated to admit it, Misha had kept his end of the bargain and saved her life.

After they landed, Misha called her a cab and told her he would meet her later at the hotel. As she was too tired to argue, she reluctantly agreed and headed to the Century Plaza Hotel in Century City. Thank goodness she had already packed her bags and Jose had her plane ticket and hotel reservations. When they got to the airport in Miami late last night, she easily changed her booking, and they left Florida on the first flight out.

Upon arrival in Los Angeles, Alex noticed the all-too-familiar gray smog covering the city, and the sun hazing through the noxious gases. As the taxi pulled off the 405 Freeway at the Santa Monica Boulevard exit, she finally saw the Century towers looming in the distance, surrounded by an enclave of high-story office and residential buildings. The cab pulled up to the hotel and Alex immediately checked in, and ran up to her room to call Miami.

Jose answered the phone after the first ring. "Dear God, child! Where are you? We've been frantic!"

"I'm sorry I left without a word, but I really didn't have much of a choice. Is Jason okay?" asked Alex.

"Yes, *mi amor*. He's going home this morning. The hospital staff has had enough of him."

"He's not very good at handling pain," Alex volunteered.

"That's putting it mildly," agreed Jose. "Where are you?"

"I'm in LA. We got on the last plane out of Miami last night. The killer was hot on our tail. We had to put some distance between us and buy some time," explained Alex. "I'm sorry I didn't call you earlier. I'm sure my mother is furious."

"She'll be fine as soon as I tell her you're okay," Jose told her. "She's a strong woman."

"I'm going to get him," said Alex. "The gala is tomorrow night and nothing is going to stop me from confronting that bastard! Not even his hired killer!"

"Do you have any proof that Heidrich hired him?" asked the editor.

"Well, it's not like I have copies of cancelled checks or anything. No, I don't have proof. Misha told me Heidrich is gunning for us and …"

"Then how do you know?" interrupted Jose. "Maybe this Misha person is playing you?"

"Well then, let's say I'm going by my journalistic instincts."

"You trust this man that much?"

"He saved my life last night."

"Hmmm. I guess war makes for strange bedfellows," Jose murmured.

Alex hung up the phone, promising to call her mother later and headed out into Century City. She needed a dress. The gala was black-tie and Alex's wardrobe was seriously lacking. She walked around the outdoor mall and entered the Versace boutique. After about a dozen different tries, she settled on a simple long, black v-neck dress with a plunging back. Satisfied with her purchase, Alex headed back to her hotel room. When she opened the door, Misha was lying on the bed, smoking a cigarette.

Alex threw her bag down and sat on the bed next to him. "Where were you?"

"I had to see a man about a gun," responded Misha, his eyes twinkling in amusement.

"Your Balkan connections have no boundaries, do they?" asked Alex, her eyes narrowing, questioning his motivations. "And, am I to assume that the gun is solely for our protection?"

Misha rose from the bed, opened the refrigerator under the wet bar and pulled out two small bottles of vodka. "Cocktail, my lady?"

"You haven't answered my question," she said as she glared angrily in Misha's direction. "I want the truth."

"Do you actually believe that there is truth in times of war?" asked Misha as he poured the vodka, handing Alex a glass.

"The war is thousands of miles away."

"That's where you're making your first mistake."

"Look, I'm too tired to play your philosophical games. I want a straight answer out of you!" Alex said, shaking her head in frustration.

"Wars lead good men to do things they would not normally do," said Misha as he downed his glass then walked back over to the bed and sat by Alex.

"So, in your bullshit cryptic fashion, you're telling me you've been lying to me. You're not just here to protect me while I finish this story on Heidrich. You're here to kill him, you bastard!" accused Alex as she flung the vodka in Misha's face and raced for the phone. "Over my dead body!"

Misha pushed her against the wall and pinned her hands by her head. He was breathing hard and his eyes turned a thousands shades of gray as his anger grew. "You stupid, foolish woman! Wake up!" he cried as he threw her into a chair by the window overlooking the busy street below. "If I don't put a stop to this then no one will! Do you actually think anyone in your government gives two shits about whether or not people are dying in Yugoslavia? Do you?"

Alex sat dumbfounded and silent as he continued his diatribe. "Do you know all my men are dead? They were all gunned down in South Beach two days ago, all five of them. Gunned down like dogs. And, do you know who's responsible yet again?"

Alex just stared at him as tears began to flow down his face.

"Heidrich!" he told her, slamming his fist on the table. "He killed five good men, and he will kill scores more. That shipment is due to arrive tomorrow or the next day, and if you don't help me stop him, you will have the blood of thousands on your hands."

Misha rose and walked to the window, keeping his back to Alex, his voice shaking as he spoke.

"Talk to me then about conscience," he said stiffly, turning to face her, his eyes on fire. "You think you have the right to sit here and judge me while you hide in your safe little glass house, experiencing war only through second-hand accounts. How fucking clean and convenient!"

He stared out at the impenetrable smog over the city. "How very American of you," he mumbled, an angry vein pulsing at his temple.

"This has nothing to do with my being American," Alex said, joining him, pressing his tear-stained face against hers, running her fingertips up his temple and along his prominent hairline. "This has to do with right and wrong. Look at me, Misha," she said, verging on hysteria.

Misha turned to face her, his eyes dark and far away, pain carving a permanent mark on his soul.

"Let me do my job," Alex said quietly. "Please. If you give me the chance to expose Heidrich then not only will he be stopped but so will others. Once this breaks open, the weight of guilt and complicity will rest on the shoulders of governments around the world. They can't hide from the evidence once it's been revealed."

"And if you don't succeed, what then?"

"I won't fail, I promise you. Trust me."

"You're using my words against me," he said, shaking his head with grim assurance.

"I've learned from a master," replied Alex, as if reading his mind.

She hoped she had won the first round, but the match was nowhere near over. The biggest challenge lay ahead. Alex needed to make sure that Heidrich lived through tomorrow night.

✵ ✵ ✵

Wilhelm Heidrich pulled up to the Beverly Hilton Hotel in his black stretch limousine, and with his personal assistant, a twenty-something, jet-lagged MBA grad, by his side, headed up to his suite grumbling in his usual fashion.

"I can't believe they actually thought I'd stay in Long Beach," Heidrich grumbled.

"Of course, I understand that, sir. But the consensus was that it would be a gracious gesture on your part if you would stay in one of their luxury hotels by the harbor to support the city, and promote the area," replied the nervous assistant.

"I've already donated enough money for them to transform their grungy oil fields into green, grassy golf courses, so I don't want to hear shit about whether I'm to stay there or not."

"Of course, sir. I'll call our city contacts and let them know that we will attend the function as scheduled tomorrow evening," his assistant said, shaking his head vigorously.

"Where is Chao staying?" asked the cranky chief executive.

"At the Beverly Hills Hotel, sir."

"You see! Even a chinaman won't stay in Long Beach!"

Heidrich's assistant was stunned into momentary silence and after a few seconds said, "Yes, sir. I'll leave your messages on the desk, and I'll go and check on tonight's dinner reservations."

Heidrich sat down and flipped through the daily newspapers before perusing his messages. One call especially caught his attention. Heidrich picked up the phone and dialed the number.

"So, you didn't get them all, did you?" he fumed.

"No," replied Aegis. "But don't worry. Their network is seriously damaged. I'll accomplish the mission by tomorrow."

"You'd better! I can't have some lunatic making a scene at the party tomorrow night."

"I assume you'll have the usual precautions in place?" asked Aegis. "You shouldn't take any chances."

"What, in case you fail again?" the chief executive taunted him.

"There are unforeseen circumstances in operations like these."

Heidrich laughed. "They would have to have a lot of balls to try to even get within a hundred yards of the *Queen Mary*. The place is not only going to be overflowing with police but also with the President's secret service guys. I'd like to see them try."

"I have everything under control, sir," Aegis assured him. "Just enjoy your evening."

"Don't disappointment me again," warned Heidrich as he hung up. He had one hour to shower and dress for dinner with Chao and his delegation.

Traffic clogged La Cienega Boulevard all the way south to the freeway. Heidrich sat in his limousine fuming, issuing complaints and then orders first to his assistant and then to the driver. Finally they pulled up in front of l'Orangerie, a posh French restaurant on the edge of Beverly Hills and West Hollywood. The Chinese delegation were already inside, drinking cocktails at their dinner table.

"Chao! It is an honor to see you again, my friend," said Heidrich as he approached the table and bowed slightly.

Chao rose and bowed and introduced the other members of his party. One was the Minister of Transport from Beijing and the three other men were executives at Shanghai Shipping. Heidrich took at seat next to Chao and ordered a dry martini.

"I hope your trip was pleasant," remarked Heidrich.

"Yes, very. We made a stop in Indonesia and then continued here. We are most pleased with how our business arrangements are progressing, and this is all due to your kind and generous friendship," Chao told him, grinning broadly. The other men at the table smiled and nodded in agreement.

"I hope our alliance will continue for many more prosperous years," said Heidrich as he lifted his glass in toast. "To Shanghai Shipping and Brand Industries!" The men at the table lifted their glasses and toasted their business partnership.

As the men reviewed the menu, Heidrich leaned over and whispered to Chao. "And, how was your meeting this morning?"

Chao smiled. "We were very honoured to have coffee with your President. We greatly value his support and yours, my friend."

Heidrich was pleased. The President had kept his promise. As the chief lobbyist for handing over the historic naval base to the Chinese, the President not only held the high-level meetings at the White House, but included none other than his Chief of Staff and the Deputy Secretary of Defense to press the City of Long Beach to go along with the deal. The National Security Council was not even asked for comment on whether giving China a base on the U.S. West Coast might possibly compromise national security. And the President had appointed a former lobbyist for the Chinese as the chief reviewer of the project. Anyway you looked at it, Heidrich had worked out a sweetheart of a deal for Beijing.

"And our shipment? Is it on course?" asked Heidrich.

"It will arrive without fail within the next two days," reassured his Chinese partner.

Heidrich sat back in his chair and looked around the restaurant. His efforts were paying off and he wasn't going to let anyone ruin what it took him years to build, least of all some small-time, would-be assassin. The pinnacle of success was within his reach.

CHAPTER TWENTY-SEVEN
TRIBUTE OF BLOOD

"It is always the best policy to speak the truth, unless, of course, you are an exceptionally good liar."
Jerome K. Jerome

Misha left Alex at the hotel and drove his rented car down to Venice Beach where he parked in front of a small, tattered bungalow on Market Street. At his third knock, Peja cautiously opened the door, peering through the crack.

"It's about time you got here," he said as he let Misha in. The older man was badly wounded. Even though the bullet hadn't lodged itself in his abdomen, Misha's amateur stitching left Peja aching and feverish, but they didn't have a choice. Emergency wards always alerted authorities if anyone showed up in need of treatment for a gunshot wound. Much to Peja's surprise, the bottle of *slivovitz* he drank prior to the procedure had knocked him out until the next day. Then the pain had set in with a vengeance.

"*Sto me boli,*" complained Peja. The painkillers weren't doing the trick, and he had hoped for something stronger, but he needed to have his wits about him. He slowly walked over to the bed and sat down, groaning as he lifted his legs onto the mattress. "*Sine moj, daj mi rakiju.* My son, give me a shot of the *slivovitz,*" he said as he pointed at the half empty bottle on the table in the corner of the small room.

"The dinner's tomorrow night, and the journalist has an interview with Heidrich at seven," Misha explained, pouring himself a drink. "She told me

169

she's already written the story, but the paper is just holding off until they have some sort of comment from him."

"So what?" Peja said. "The story is just a way for you to get near that Nazi bastard. Why are you telling me all this?"

"Don't you think that his judgment in front of the world would serve our interests even more?" volunteered the young Serb.

"What! Are you fucking kidding me?" Peja demanded, his face turning scarlet. "Your mission is clear!"

"I know we originally came here to …" continued Misha, feebly.

"*Dosta*! What are you talking about?" Peja yelled. "What happened to my warrior? You're sounding like some United Nations flunky!"

He tried rising from the bed, but clearly the pain was too great.

"What has she done to you, Misha?" Peja was pleading now. "What in God's name has she done to you?"

"Nothing! She's done nothing to me. It's just that it may serve our purposes even more if she exposes him and we return to Bosnia now and continue the fight," Misha explained. He couldn't look the older man in the eye. It was as though the words coming out of his mouth weren't his own.

"Coward! Just because we lost one battle doesn't mean we turn and run!"

"I'm not running from anything. Ever," the younger man protested.

Peja rolled to the edge of the bed and grabbed Misha's arm. "Don't you remember the story of the Aga returning to our villages with his fully armed escort, coming to collect our male children for the blood tribute?" he demanded. "Don't you remember anything?"

Misha remembered the stories his parents told him of how the Turks had chosen the healthiest, brightest and best-looking Serbian boys between ten and fifteen years old and forced them onto a long convoy bound for the Muslim empire. They carried these boys off as their mothers sat begging and pleading then wailing and praying as though they were at a funeral. Following these caravans until their bodies gave out, the women watched as the river took their children away to a land where they were circumcised, where they were taught to forget their faith, their country and their origin, and even to forget their mothers in the name of Islam. For most Serbian children, this was a story that nightmares were made of.

Peja continued talking, his voice full of fury. "You bring shame to our brothers and sisters who fled to the hills and mountains and organized to challenge Hitler's might and to fight the *Ustashe* and the Muslim fundamentalists who aligned with the Nazis," he told Misha. "They killed

800,000 of our own people and you dare stand here and tell me that this man should be brought before a bullshit tribunal and go off and spend the rest of his days in some luxury prison! For shame!"

Misha was speechless. For a warrior nation, there was no greater crime than collaboration with the enemy, and Peja was accusing him of that.

"You actually think that that sham of an organization called the United Nations will actually protect our people, our land? No! There is no higher authority than God and he has spoken to us now as he has over the centuries," Peja said. "Don't be sucked into their lies. This man, Heidrich, and his kind need to be stopped. He needs to pay for his past sins, and we have a duty to prevent him from committing others."

"Forgive me," said Misha as he lowered his head. "You're right. I've been a fool to even consider such an option."

Peja leaned over and grabbed Misha's face between his hands. "No more talk then of misguided mercy," he ordered. "It's all set for tomorrow. Our people will get you on the *Queen Mary* in plenty of time to finish him off. Now go and prepare yourself for judgment day."

"It will be done," Misha whispered. "I swear to you, Peja, it will be done."

As the young Serb stepped out into the crisp Los Angeles night, he caught his breath then crossed himself. His lips trembled as he whispered a prayer. Somehow he knew that he would never see his homeland again.

CHAPTER TWENTY-EIGHT
THE INGLORIOUS END

"All men love peace in their armchairs after dinner; but they disbelieve the other nations' professions, rightly measuring its sincerity by their own."
Oscar W. Firkins

Alex stood examining herself in the bathroom mirror, having carefully applied her makeup and put her long brunette hair into a chignon at the base of her neck. She dressed slowly as though she were heading out on a date, but her engagement tonight was with a killer.

She had spent most of the day preparing her notes for the interview, and even checked the batteries in her cassette recorder. Alex was nervous. After all these weeks of murder and mayhem, she was finally going to confront the man responsible for it all. She called downstairs and asked the hotel concierge to arrange for a car to take her to Long Beach.

Grabbing her press credentials, she headed out the door. The driver waited outside the hotel, and immediately they left to try to avoid the heaviest traffic on the 405 Freeway. As they approached the end of the Long Beach Freeway, Alex saw the drydocked oceanliner tied at the water front, beaming in majestic lights. It was an unbelievable sight, Alex thought as they pulled up to the security area where they checked her credentials before ushering her through.

Music flowed down from the upper decks of the *Queen Mary* as Alex headed to the boarding ramp, decorated with Chinese lanterns and dragons.

The gala had already started and many of the select invitees were already on board, sampling hors d'oeuvres and sipping champagne. Once on the ship, she walked to the information booth and asked for the press attaché.

"Alexandra Miletic with *The Miami Gazette*. I'm here for a scheduled interview with Wilhelm Heidrich," she said as she pulled out her press pass. She was escorted to the old First Class lounge, now known as the Queen's Salon.

As Alex walked through the ship, she was mesmerized by her grandeur. She had done her homework and she knew that the *Queen Mary* had been conceived in the late 1920s as the first of a pair of 1,000 foot long ships intended to provide regularly scheduled weekly service between Southampton, England and New York City and that, on Her Majesty's sixty-ninth birthday, the glorious "floating city" was presented as a gift to Queen Mary of England. Stretching more than 1,000 feet in length and weighing more than 77,500 tons, the *Queen Mary* was the flagship of the Cunard White Star Line, and made many record-breaking journeys across the Atlantic.

During WWII, the ship was converted for use as a troop transport vessel, and spent six years transporting over 800,000 British soldiers. Her voyages were so valued that British Prime Minister Winston Churchill credited the vessel with shortening the war by as much as a year.

After the war the *Queen Mary* had transported troops home as well as war brides and their babies from Britain to the United States and Canada, and then continued as a passenger ship until retirement when she was purchased by the City of Long Beach in 1967. Flush with tideland oil money, the city had bought the majestic vessel and turned her into a tourist attraction including a hotel, convention center and museum. To Alex, it seemed way too Disneylike, and she wondered how the ghosts of this grand ship felt, knowing this magnificent relic was on commercial display in a modern-day circus-like atmosphere, placing her courageous history alongside the achievements of Mickey Mouse and Donald Duck.

Alex continued to admire the *Queen Mary* as she followed her escort to the Queen's Salon, where Wilhelm Heidrich was holding court. He sat behind a beautiful, hand-carved antique desk, surrounded by a number of Chinese delegates and the Republican Senator of California. They looked up as she entered.

"You must be Alexandra Miletic," said Heidrich as he rose and approached her, his hand extended. "Always a pleasure to meet a member of our illustrious press brigade."

Alex stared into his hollow blue eyes for what seemed to be the better part of a minute. *So, this is what a mass murderer looks like*, she thought as she briefly shook his hand, disguising her disgust.

"I was thinking that we might take a stroll around the ship while we chatted," Heidrich suggested as he placed his hand on her naked back, his ice-cold fingers sending a terrifying chill up her spine. "The crew has been telling me some interesting tales about this grand lady."

As they walked along the first class deck, Alex noted that two brawny bodyguards kept five feet behind them, their eyes on alert for any potential threat.

"I've read some fascinating stories of ghost sightings," said Alex as Heidrich took two glasses of champagne from the tray which a waiter was carrying by.

"Since it adds to the historic mystique of the ship," Heidrich said as he sipped at his champagne, "I'm sure those stories assist the sales people in booking the hotel."

"You don't believe in ghosts then?" asked Alex, eyeing his long manicured hands. He was as slick as a major oil spill, and just as deadly.

"Let's say I'm more involved in the here and now."

"Did you know that the onboard crew regularly hears inexplicable pounding sounds near the Bosun's Locker, which is the area of the hull that sliced the Light Cruiser Curacoa in half during World War II?" Alex asked him. She wanted to keep him off balance, setting the stage for her *grande finale*. And, apparently her tactic was working. Heidrich glanced uneasily around him, his right eye slightly twitching.

"Apparently, due to her wartime sailing orders, the *Queen Mary* was not allowed to stop to rescue survivors, and 338 men perished in the cold ocean," she said, without skipping a beat. "You haven't by any chance heard the disembodied voices of the victims as you walked through the passageways, have you?"

"No, I haven't," said Heidrich, his eyes narrowing into two slits.

"And I hear that poltergeist activity has been reported in the kitchen, where a cook was murdered during World War II," Alex continued ruthlessly. "It is said his cooking was so terrible that it caused a riot among troops being carried to the front. The violence apparently got so out of hand that the cook ended up stuffed inside an oven and burned to death. Somehow his ghastly screams were impregnated into the ship's iron bulkhead."

Alex broke off and stared directly into his cruel-looking face. "Do you believe that the dead come back seeking justice for wrongs that were committed against them, Mr. Heidrich?"

"No, I don't," responded Heidrich, clearly enraged with the line of questioning. "And if you don't mind my asking, Miss Miletic, what does this have to do with our subject for the evening? I was told we were to discuss the economic redevelopment of Long Beach. "

"Of course," replied Alex as she pointed to a table and chairs on the upper deck of the ship. "Shall we?" she asked as they walked over and sat down. Alex pulled out her tiny tape recorder and pressed the record button, "You don't mind, do you?"

Heidrich shook his head after searching Alex's eyes for warning signs. "Of course not. Please proceed."

"We were about to discuss economic redevelopment," she said. "So, kindly tell our readers if you would, why you became a proponent of the leasing of the historic naval base to the Chinese?"

"Well," he replied without hesitation. "The world has dramatically changed since the fall of the Berlin Wall, and opportunities abound to create new and long reaching friendships. We were faced with an overabundance of bases, and no external threats to justify their existence. So, from a business standpoint, we needed to diversify our holdings and divest ourselves of non-performing assets."

"Of course, Mr. Heidrich," Alex said, maintaining her best professional crispness. "We understand the theory behind the base closings, but what most interests our readers is how a critical U.S. port facility ended up in the hands of the Chinese? Is it not a matter of national security that a major port of entry is controlled by Shanghai Shipping, given their deplorable record including arms smuggling, chemical weapons transport in the Persian Gulf, violation of U.S. shipping law in connection with its practices involving bribery of government officials, violations of international safety regulations, and violations of international environmental regulations against dumping some 640 tons of raw waste into the open sea. Of course," Alex added, "I'm naming just a few."

Heidrich glared at her, his index finger crossed his thin lips as if asking for silence.

"And, how is it, sir, that in exchange for this naval base, the Chinese have agreed to work with you and Brand Industries to transport arms and ammunitions to the Bosnian Muslims and the *mujahadeen*, for a hefty profit, I assume, in violation of the international arms embargo to the war torn region of Yugoslavia? Are you also not being paid by some very questionable Middle East financiers with ties to terrorist organizations?"

Heidrich rose and slowly placed his empty champagne glass down on the table. "This interview is over," he said, his face expressionless.

"And, Mr. Heidrich," Alex said defiantly, hounding him as he hurriedly walked away down the ship's passageway. "How is that, after fifty years you are still thriving despite the fact that you committed atrocities during World War II?"

She dogged his steps as he hurried along the deck, holding the tape recorder high above her head.

"*Herr* Heidrich," she persisted, "How did a Nazi like you get to become a leader of the American business community? Tell our readers about Operation Bloodstone and how the U.S. government sold its soul to the Devil when it brought you and your kind onto our soil!"

He stopped and turned to face Alex as his body guards stepped in to prevent her from coming closer. "You have nothing on me, and you know it," he said in a low voice before turning on his heel and marching down the stairs towards the grand ballroom.

Alex's heart felt ready to burst from her chest. She caught her breath as she stared at the Long Beach harbor lights, and turned off her tape recorder.

"Give me strength, *teta*," said Alex as she headed to the reception, absolutely certain she was way in over her head. But, she wasn't through with Heidrich yet.

Entering the main deck of the ship, she approached the grand ballroom. Both American and Chinese dignitaries in formal dress milled about the entrance, waiting for security to clear them to enter the Presidential Gala. Alex noticed secret service men surveying the crowd, their eyes darting about the crowd, talking into their headsets. The President was due to arrive in any minute.

Alex presented her invitation and press pass and was ushered into an elegant room containing several hundred round tables, beautifully decorated with flower centerpieces and Chinese regalia. At the front of the room was a long table for the honorees, including the Chinese delegation, Long Beach officials, and Heidrich and his Brand Industries cronies.

Alex found her seating card on a table at the back of the room, near the door to the kitchen. She took her seat beside the only guest at the table, a drunk, heavyset man with a Southern accent.

"Would you like an olive, little missie?" her dinner companion asked her as he passed the plate of hors d'oeuvres.

"No thank you," responded Alex as her eyes searched for Heidrich. She found him at the front standing next to the Deputy Secretary of Defense and a Chinese man she didn't recognize.

"I just flew in special for this shin-ding," the drunk man continued. "That President of ours is exactly what this country needs. Don't you agree?"

"No man can serve two masters," muttered Alex, staring as Heidrich approached the microphone to introduce the President.

"Damn little lady. You may be right," he laughed heartily. "I suppose that's politics for ya," said the man as he lifted his glass in toast. "Welcome to Babylon!"

Alex watched as the President of the United States walked into the grand ballroom, surrounded by secret service men. He walked up to the small stage and shook hands with the members of the various delegation, then stopped and hugged Heidrich.

Suddenly the lights dimmed, and Heidrich walked over to the microphone to introduce the President.

"Ladies and gentlemen, it is my distinct honor to present to you tonight, a man who needs no introduction, a man who has devoted his whole life to our country, a man who will go down in history as a beacon of light in times of trouble. Ladies and gentlemen, I give you, the President of the United States of America." Heidrich moved away from the podium as he shook the President's hand and took his seat at the table of honorees.

"Good evening, my friends, my fellow Americans, and our new friends who have traveled far to be with us tonight," said the President as he looked around the room. "This is an historic night. We are here to celebrate the coming of a new dawn. For too many years, the nations of the world have been separated by differences, but as we approach the 21st century, we will be united in a common goal. And, I'm here tonight to speak of that common goal, a goal that will leave our children with a legacy they can be proud of, a legacy of peace and mutual cooperation.

"The United States has an obligation as the leader of the free world to continue its vigilant campaign to combat the evils that threaten to disrupt our New World Order. With our brave men and women at the helm, we will achieve that goal. And with our friends around the world, we will achieve peace in our lifetime.

"From our birth, America has always been more than just a place. America has embodied an idea that has become the ideal for billions of people throughout the world. Our founders said it best: America is about life, liberty and the pursuit of happiness. Today, because of our dedication, America's ideals—liberty, democracy and peace—are more and more the aspirations of people everywhere in the world. It is the power of our ideas, even more than our size, our wealth and our military might, that makes America a uniquely trusted nation.

"We must not idly stand by while countries struggle to capture the democratic dream. We must provide as much support as is necessary to rebuild and form democratic nations. We will achieve peace in Central Europe. Securing peace in Bosnia will also help to build a free and stable Europe. Bosnia lies at the very heart of Europe, next door to many of its fragile new democracies and some of our closest allies. Generations of Americans have understood that Europe's freedom and Europe's stability is vital to our own national security. In Bosnia, this terrible war has challenged our interests and troubled our souls. Thankfully, we can do something about it. I say again our mission will be clear, limited, and achievable. The people of Bosnia, our NATO allies, and people all around the world are now looking to America for leadership, so let us lead. That is our responsibility as Americans. I thank you all and God bless America."

The crowd rose and gave the President a standing ovation while Alex remained in her seat, dumbfounded. She was amazed at how the leader of this nation had just packed two solid punches into one speech. Not only did he not mention the agreement with Shanghai Shipping, but he brought the whole Yugoslav conflict onto the agenda. Tonight had played into his own political maneuvering.

For months, the President had been trying to drum up support to lift the arms embargo, but had kept hitting a brick wall with Congress. No elected figure was ready to take responsibility for the massive influx of arms that would invariably flow into the war zone. Obviously, the President had realized that he had to take a different tactic, and instead, lobby the American public for support. She had just witnessed the beginning of his campaign.

Alex turned and saw the confused and disappointed look on the Chinese delegates' faces as the President declined to be photographed with them and hurriedly left the ballroom. A shrewd politician, he also must have known that having his face plastered in all the papers, shaking hands with the Chinese over the naval base lease would have been political suicide.

Too low key, yet, as Alex knew, this blatant example of cheap political wheeling and dealing did not bode well for the world. She needed to act.

She watched as Heidrich glad-handed his way about the room, and then, quite suddenly, disappeared in the direction of the upper deck. Alex followed him as she turned on her tape recorder. She found him standing by the rail of the ship, sipping champagne, his bodyguards a few feet away. They moved to prevent her from getting closer, until Heidrich lifted his hand and said, "It's okay, boys."

"You have a lot of balls for a woman," he told her as the bright decorative lights danced on his glistening gray temples. The lights illuminated his narrow, austere face, allowing Alex to look into the depths of what she believed to be the epitome of evil.

"My gender has nothing to do with it," replied Alex as she pulled out a cigarette and lit it. "I'm going to bring you down," she said calmly.

Heidrich threw his head back and laughed. "You and what army?" He turned and started walking away, humming some tune from the past.

Suddenly, Heidrich froze. Shots rang out hitting one of his men in the chest and the other in the head. They both fell down dead at his feet, their guns still in their holsters.

Alex dove for cover behind an old life raft, ducking as she listened to the echo of the gunshots still playing off the highrise buildings in the harbor. As she peeked out from behind her cover, she saw Misha standing face to face with Heidrich.

Quickly scrambling to her feet, she started running towards them. "No!" she yelled.

Misha looked in her direction and smiled.

"*Molim te, nemoj!*" Please don't do it! screamed Alex.

He hesitated slightly then aimed the gun point blank at Heidrich's head.

"You think you have the right to judge me, you Serbian dog," snarled Heidrich. He stood defying his assassin. "Death to all of you," he added as he spat in Misha's face.

"The only one who's going to judge you is God," Misha said as he cocked his weapon. "You should have died a long time ago, *Herr General.*"

"You pathetic swine! You have no authority over me!" screamed Heidrich as he took a few steps back, stumbling as he retreated.

"*Za sve pravoslavne duse,*" murmured Misha as he crossed himself and took aim. On behalf of all the Orthodox souls.

"No, Misha!"

Alex was a few feet from them when the sound of a bullet pierced the silent night air. She stopped dead in her tracks. Heidrich turned and ran down the stairs as Misha stood standing for a few seconds then slid down along the railing, his chest bloodied. Alex ran up to him and tore open his shirt to examine the wound.

"God, I think it's bad!" said Alex as she held his hand in hers. Misha's eyelids began to flutter as he labored to breathe. He was starting to turn blue, drowning in his own blood.

"You weren't supposed to be here. You promised me," Alex whispered as she stroked his dark curls.

"I couldn't live with myself if I didn't die a warrior's death," said Misha as Alex forced back tears.

"Don't cry, my lady. Bring me cold water from the well and wash my burning brow and pour me wine, red wine, for I have thirst. I am sorely wounded, and my heart is bloodless now," he whispered as he stared into Alex's eyes. The few passages of the famous Serbian poem were his final words as died in Alex's arms.

As she cradled his body, Alex heard footsteps behind her. She lifted her head and saw a figure approaching from the other side of the passageway. Aegis stood a few feet away, pointing his gun at her.

Gently, Alex laid Misha's head down and rose to her feet aware, for the first time that she was covered in blood.

"My, my, aren't you a sight," whispered Aegis. "You look almost too good to kill."

"Look," she told him, taking a few slow steps back. "We can work this out. I know that Heidrich hired you and if you agree to testify against him, then I'm sure the court ..."

"Shhh," said Aegis softly. He aimed the gun as he blew her a kiss. "Just say goodnight, darling."

Alex closed her eyes and saw Teta Maria smiling at her. "Don't be afraid, *macane*," said her aunt's apparition. "I'm always with you."

She started to pray. *Hail Mary, full of grace ... oh, God*, thought Alex, she'd forgotten the words! She shut her eyes even tighter. There are no atheists in a foxhole.

After what seemed to be an eternity, the shot rang out. Alex felt nothing, only the beating of her own heart, and then she heard a groan and a loud splash in the water below. Slowly, fearfully, she opened her eyes. The killer was gone and Agent Sommett was standing five yards away.

"I told you I'd protect you, baby girl," said the FBI agent as he replaced his weapon in his shoulder holster.

A team of paramedics had arrived and were performing CPR on Misha. Alex ran over and dropped to her knees beside him. "Can you save him?" she asked frantically.

"He's gone, Alex," said Sommett as he stood over her. "Let them finish their jobs."

Sommett grabbed Alex and lead her away as the paramedics were packing away the electrocardiogram, and a white sheet was placed over the corpse.

Alex brushed away his grip, ran over to the railing and looked below. A police boat was already fishing Aegis's body out of the murky water.

A sea of people rushed about on the dock and Alex caught sight of Heidrich's gray hair, shimmering in the search lights. He was being directed into a limousine by his entourage. Heidrich hesitated for a moment and looked up to catch Alex's gaze. He smiled as his men ushered him into the vehicle. The car sped away.

"You can't let him get away!" demanded Alex.

"I have nothing on him," replied the agent as he put a blanket around her shoulders. "Let's go inside."

"He killed Misha!" protested Alex. "He almost killed me!"

"Alex listen to me. You have no proof."

"Like hell! His assassin is lying on that boat right now," said Alex. She pointed to a police cruiser that just docked. Officials had arrived and were headed over with a stretcher to transport the body to the County Coroner's Office.

"Dead men don't talk," said Sommett, shaking his head.

Alex's eyes combed the deck. "Where's my purse?" she said. "I have everything on tape." The sirens wailed in the distance as she fell to her knees and started crawling, checking under the life raft and the tables. Her purse was nowhere in sight.

"This is a crime scene," Sommett advised her as he forcefully directed her down the stairs and into a cabin below deck. "Everything is being gathered by our forensics specialists and is considered evidence. You'll get it back."

"There is no tape, right?" asked Alex softly as she took a seat by the portal window.

Sommett didn't respond.

"You're just going to turn a blind eye to all of this, aren't you?" asked Alex disbelievingly. Her blood froze in her veins.

"It's over now," Sommett said, his face expressionless. "We found the killer."

"You're letting the biggest criminal get away! What about Bloodstone and the arms shipments, and the truth?" pleaded Alex, pounding her fists as hard as she could against the wall.

"The truth can't come out," he told her, his eyes serious as he delivered what Alex knew must be his official speech. "At least not now. As far as the shipments go, well, if it doesn't reach Bosnia, the Muslims will get slaughtered. We're just leveling the playing field."

"Give me a break!" she told him. "You don't give a crap about the Muslims!"

"Maybe not," the agent said stiffly. "But we do care about stability in the region and we can't let the killing continue in Bosnia. The problem is we can't be on the up and up about it. In a year or so, Congress will lift the arms embargo and then what weve done will only be regarded as a secret humanitarian effort. Nothing more and nothing less."

The truth was hard to swallow. "And you can sleep at night?" asked Alex feebly as her throat tightened.

"It's all part of a zero-sum game, baby girl," said Agent Sommett as he turned and left her alone in the cabin.

She curled her knees under her chin then reached for the phone. Sommett was wrong. It wasn't over. She still had a story to file.

CHAPTER TWENTY–NINE
A TIME OF DEATH

"The pure and simple truth is rarely pure and never simple."
Oscar Wilde

"All grace be to Allah, *alhamdulillah*," said the *mujahadeen* leader as the he sat on the hill watching the freighter approach the empty docking area. The darkened hull of the ship broke eerily through the early evening mist, appearing more as a long-lost ghost vessel than a freighter of goods. He watched as the ship's search lights quickly turned on and off three times, signaling their onshore contact.

The Islamic fighter rose to his feet and motioned to his men to move the caravan of trucks down from the tree-covered slopes towards the teal green Adriatic Sea, and to the makeshift unloading dock below. They had very little time to unload and head for the dangerous road from Dubrovnik to Trebinje, Bosnia where they were to meet with three other *mujahadeen* brigades.

Dubrovnik sat under the bare limestone mass of Monte Sergio on a ridge which jutted out into the Adriatic Sea. The city's seaward fortifications rose directly from the water's edge, standing boldly on a tall rock almost isolated by a little inlet of the Adriatic. The majestic medieval city wasn't dead, but comatose as the convoy of trucks rumbled through. The few remaining shutters on the bombed out hillside homes remained closed as the trucks rumbled through the narrow cobblestone streets. After weeks under siege, the citizens were licking their wounds, hiding from the reality of war that still controlled this mostly Croatian enclave.

The Islamic fighter knew his presence was unwelcomed. Neither the Croats nor the few Serbs who still remained in the area tolerated the presence of his fundamentalist army. *Christians and Jews would never be satisfied with the Muslims until they followed the Christian or Judaic ways,* he mused. His men needed to move out quickly.

Since the early summer, the Bosnian Muslim troops had been consistently reinforced by 'volunteers' from the ranks of several Islamic organizations. These fundamentalist Muslim fighters had arrived in Bosnia in answer to Tehran's call to fight the Jihad, the Holy War, eager to commit martyrdom in the name of Islam. They included highly trained and combat-proven volunteers from Iran, Afghanistan, Lebanon and several other Arab countries. Most of the Arab fighters had previously fought in the ranks of Palestinian terrorist organizations in Lebanon and in the resistance in Afghanistan with the Taliban.

The Islamic fighter had arrived to Bosnia seeking martyrdom. He came wanting the word of Allah to be supreme and the word of the disbelievers to be low and despised. All he and his fighters wished for was for a bullet to take them to *Shahada* to bear witness to the existence and unity of God.

After the conquest of Kabul, the holy warrior had thanked Allah, proclaiming that his heart was overcome by the joy of Jihad. He believed in the Prophet's word that "the highest peak of Islam is Jihad," and he was looking for another war to wage. Many of his fighters had continued the battle against the infidels in the Philippines and in Kashmir, but he had chosen to start a new Jihad in Bosnia, believing that the Prophet of Islam placed peace and blessings upon those who continued the holy war until the day of judgment. Only fifteen days had lapsed between the conquest of Kabul and the day when he was called to his mission in Bosnia where he formed a new battalion under a unified command called Kateebat al-Mujahideen with which they had fought alongside the Bosnian army in defense of Islam and their fellow Muslims in the region.

Although he had claimed it was not his view, he said that his Muslim brethren told him the war was not an *Azmah* or crisis but rather a *Rahmah* or a blessing. He and his fighters believed that if it were not for them, the Bosnian Muslims would not have known Allah, and would not have found the road to the Mosque. He saw loose Western morals corrupting his brothers and sisters everywhere until it was difficult to tell a Muslim from a Christian. The Muslim women were *Kasiyat-Ariyat* or exposed, but since the arrival of him and his men, their women were beginning to once again wear the complete

Hijab', proudly parading in the market or on the streets covering their body and faces. The commitment to Islamic religious doctrine and the return to Allah was growing quickly in the midst of all the terror.

The mujahadeen leader jumped out of his jeep, and ordered his men to board the ship. He stood watching as the cargo hull was emptied of the tons of crates of weaponry destined for use against the army of infidels.

Stroking his henna-colored long beard, he watched as the sun began to rise. The Islamic fighter faced Mecca and praised the day. "All grace be to Allah, as is due unto Him, and I bear witness that there is no one worthy of worship except Allah and that Muhammad is his slave and messenger." Then the trucks headed down the bombed out road out of town, towards Bosnia and their next Holy War.

CHAPTER THIRTY
LIFE AND TIMES

"We have met the enemy and it is us."
Walt Kelly

Alex's ears finally popped as she sat in the back of the taxi, heading to the Miami Gazette building. She was chewing gum, hoping to relieve the pressure in her aural cavity from the rough descent into Miami International Airport. The editorial meeting was in an hour, and she was tense. Jose was pulling in the managing editor and the newspaper's in-house attorney to review her story. But there was one problem. Alex hadn't told Jose that the FBI had confiscated her tape.

As she left the elevator, she saw them all gathered outside the large conference room at the far end of the editorial floor.

"There she is," said Jose as he waved. "Welcome back." Alex briefly hesitated before continuing down the hallway. She recognized a look in her editor's eye that she didn't like. She was in for trouble.

When they finally closed the door, the mood changed. "You've created quite a stir in California," said Alan Crenshaw, the managing editor, as he spread out a pile of papers in front of him. "Let's see, we've had calls from the Long Beach Police, the Coroners Office, the State Attorney's Office, the FBI, and am I forgetting anyone?" he asked as perked his eyebrows and stared at the others seated at the table. "Oh, yes. I shouldn't forget the President's Chief of Staff!"

"Well, things didn't exactly go as planned," mumbled Alex. She was in really deep trouble.

"I should say not, young lady," Alan admonished as he pulled out the papers from his file. "Let's see here. You've accused Wilhelm Heidrich, one of America's top business leaders of being a Nazi. Is that correct?" he asked.

"Yes, and I ..."

"And, not only that. According to you, he and a number of his 'associates' were secretly heralded out of Europe after the war, given new identities and all under the protection and support of the U.S. Government. Is that correct?"

"Yes, but let me explain ..."

"I'm not finished," scolded Crenshaw. "So they've been here for some fifty years now, hiding the whole time under auspices of very public personas, and have for the last few years been running illegal arms shipments to countries and/or terrorist groups who have been cited as American enemies or threats to our national security. Is that correct?"

Alex just nodded. "I didn't mention that Heidrich had hired a contract killer to kill me and my source."

"Of course, forgive me. This source of yours. He was gunned down by the FBI as he was trying to assassinate Mr. Heidrich," Crenshaw said between clenched teeth, slamming the file shut. "You run around with some very questionable characters, Alex."

"But, he wasn't shot by the FBI," she protested. "He was killed by Heidrich's man. The body they fished out of the water ..."

"Alex, we've checked with the authorities and they have no record of any other so-called assassin," replied the managing editor.

"But, that's not possible!" Alex told him. "Speak to Agent Sommett, he'll confirm ..."

"We've read your story, Ms. Miletic," interrupted Peter Sloan, the attorney for the paper, "And, we've all come to the conclusion that you've dangerously crossed the borders of libel."

"Libel? You've got to be joking!" cried Alex as she looked to Jose for support. "Didn't you show them all the documents?"

Jose looked like he'd just been through the ringer. His eyes were bloodshot and his skin was sickly pale. "Tell us you kept copies."

"No. You put them in your safe," replied Alex as tears welled in her eyes. They were nailing the coffin shut.

"Well, these so called documents don't exist," chimed in the managing editor. "I assume you've gathered other supporting evidence to back up your claims."

Alex panicked. "I had a tape but it was confiscated by the FBI," she said in a low voice.

"That really complicates matters," the attorney muttered as he sat furiously taking notes. "We've been bombarded all day by Wilhelm Heidrich's attorneys threatening to sue the paper if we publish what they deem to be fabricated lies on your part. And, you're up to your ears in potential charges that include harassment, slander, aiding and abetting a criminal and a slew of other felonies."

"I assume you have something to say for yourself?" asked Crenshaw in a way which told Alex that he was sharpening the guillotine to make her death as painless as possible.

"Sir, I ..."

"Look, we know you've just had a major crisis in your life with the loss of your aunt, and we're willing to hold your job until you get well again."

Damn him! He was accusing her of being mentally unstable.

"Our human resources staff will help you get the treatment that you need," said the managing editor as he rose to leave.

"But, the story is true!" protested Alex.

"There is no story, Alex," said the attorney decisively as he stared at her from behind his wire-rimmed reading glasses. "I'm going to do the best I can with Heidrich's attorneys to get you off the hook. I don't think they'd want this to go to court, given your condition and all, but you need to stop your ravings."

Alex watched as Crenshaw and Sloan gathered their papers and left the room. She sat staring in disbelief at Jose.

"What the hell happened?" screamed Alex, but she already had a pretty good idea. It was all starting to make sense. "Where are the documents?"

Jose walked over and sat beside her, placing his hand on her shoulder. "They're gone. I don't know how, but they've just disappeared," he said. "I'm sorry."

Alex walked to the big window overlooking Biscayne Bay and looked onto the city that she loved. It finally dawned on her that she had placed her trust into too many hands. The government wasn't about to let her spill the beans on Bloodstone nor the arms shipments.

"It's not your fault," said Alex as she turned to face Jose. "They just played us."

"Mi *amor*, this isn't the first time that governments and presidents have led the public astray," said Jose, as he turned a sorrowful gaze at Alex. "Truman lied to the nation about the war in Korea, saying we were fighting for democracy even though he was asking us to support a military dictatorship."

He took a deep breath and Alex saw how exhausted he looked. "Dwight D. Eisenhower lied about our spy flights over the Soviet Union and the U.S. involvement in the coup that overthrew a democratic government in Guatemala." He went on as though he were reciting a litany. "Eisenhower deceived us about the U.S. role in subverting a government in Iran all because our oil multinationals weren't happy with the powers that be, so we put the Shah of Iran back on the throne, and his secret police tortured and executed thousands of his opponents. So much for regime change in the name of freedom!"

Alex could not believe that she was hearing her mentor rattle off like a conspiracy theorist. If she hadn't witnessed the latest injustice and coverup first-hand, she never would have believed her government capable of such deception. "John F. Kennedy lied about U.S. involvement in the 1961 failed invasion of Cuba, saying the U.S. had no intention of using military force to overthrow Castro and his government. Kennedy, Johnson, and Nixon all lied about what was happening in Vietnam, and both Johnson and Nixon lied when they claimed only military targets were bombed during the war. Oh, let's not forget that Nixon deceived the nation about the secret bombing of Cambodia and his CIA orchestrated the coup in Chile that overthrew Salvador Allende and put that murderer Pinochet in power."

The words were tumbling out of Jose now as though he no longer cared what he was saying. "Don't even get me started on Reagan and the Iran-Contra affair. Our illustrious former-actor-turned-world-leader also lied about the importance of Grenada in order to justify our 1983 invasion of that small country. George Bush lied about the reasons for invading Panama in 1989, saying it was to stop the drug trade while, in fact, Noriega was just another CIA-backed dictator who wasn't following orders to the T. Bush also deceived the nation about his real interest in the Persian Gulf. He pretended to be anguished about the fate of Kuwait while he was actually more concerned about enhancing American power in Saudi Arabia and controlling the region's oil deposits."

He paused for a breath. "I could go on and on," he said wearily, "But the bottom line is if our government has lost some sense of moral proportion, it's not new. They all lied in some form or another as they orchestrated their splendid little wars."

"It doesn't make it any easier to swallow," replied Alex, moving closer to him, and placing her hand on his shoulder.

"I'm just grateful that you didn't end up dead." Jose told her, patting her hand.

"Sommett may have saved my life, but he ruined my career," Alex told him. "That bastard stole those documents back!"

Jose looked at her, his wise eyes drawn from the stress. "Maybe he thought it was a fair trade-off."

Alex looked disgusted. "In the end, David doesn't beat Goliath. That's only a story in the Bible," she mumbled as she placed her head in her hands. "I'm through, aren't I?"

"*Mi amor*, they had such a hard time believing it in the first place. And now we have nothing to back up your claims," Jose explained. "Their hands are tied."

"Should I pack up my desk?" Alex asked him.

Jose nodded. "At least for the time being."

"It was a hell of a story, huh?" asked Alex as she grabbed her purse and walked to the door.

"You bet, *mi hija*. It was a hell of a great story."

CHAPTER THIRTY-ONE
THE GRAINS OF SAND

"Sometimes the heart sees what is invisible to the eye."
H. Jackson Brown, Jr.

Alex saw a tall, lanky figure dressed all in black standing in the driveway as she pulled up and stopped the engine. She stared at her mother's face, more serious than she had ever seen it, and struggled to hold back the tears.

Zvona's eyes said it all as she cradled Alex in her bosom, swaying gently to an ancient Croatian melody she hummed in her daughter's ear. "Welcome home, *macane*," she murmured.

"It's great to be back," Alex said, clinging to her mother as a wave of gratitude swept over her.

Jose had asked to come along for the reunion, and Alex watched as he put his hand on Zvona's waist. The three of them walked into the house, arm in arm.

"*Je si gladna?*" asked her mother. Are you hungry?

As though there was no need for her to wait for an answer, her mother strolled into the kitchen and began preparing one of her daughter's favorite dishes—hamburger and French fries. "Medium-rare, right?" checked Zvona as she banged the pots in search of the skillet.

"Like always, Mom."

Jose brought her a stiff shot of *slivovitz* and they headed out into the backyard. Alex looked at the sky and saw the clouds dancing in the heavens as the sun painted the horizon a glorious red and orange.

"It's beautiful, isn't it?" asked Alex.

"Yes, *mi bonita*, life is beautiful."

"So this is what a scapegoat feels like," Alex went on. "It kind of sucks."

"You're a brave woman, *mi amor*. You fought a valiant battle, a battle that most would shy away from. Perhaps something good can come out of all of this and we can go back to normal," Jose responded, half believing his own words.

Alex shook her head. "There's no going back, you realize that, don't you?"

"Perhaps, *mi hija*," he said, his vibrant eyes dancing in the fading Florida sunlight. "But we can move forward and try to create a better world," he added emphatically as he turned and walked back into the kitchen. Alex watched as he gently placed a kiss on Zvona's cheek then began flipping patties onto the grill.

For the first time in her life, Alex felt much like the mythological Phoenix bird spreading her wings and rising from the ashes. She had learned that the world was not black and white. There were no good guys and bad guys. There was only a shade of gray that tempted everyone to move beyond their own humanity in the name of self preservation. Up until a few weeks ago, the war was in another part of the world, far, far away. The voices of the disenfranchised fell on deaf ears, their pleas twisted and turned and finally rendered mute by governments and lapdog media organizations too absorbed in their own self interest to speak the truth. But, somehow, after all of this, God still wanted her to continue the journey.

Alex sat on a wrought iron bench and looked at the earth, washed clean from the day's rain, and reflected on her new calling. The world desperately needed to embrace a champion of truth.

Although Misha was gone, she somehow felt his spirit still around her, beckoning her to continue the fight, challenging her to expose the truth, encouraging her to do what was right regardless of the formidable foes threatening to block her path.

Alex hoped Misha was with his mother as one day she would be with Teta Maria and her father. She needed to celebrate the gifts of life, and honor those who sacrificed themselves so that she could rejoice in the daily blessings that surrounded her every day. And now, more than ever, she knew that there was enough room in her heart to love.

Alex stared at the sun as its final rays disappeared behind Miami's skyline. The wind picked up offshore and Alex thought she heard Teta

Maria's voice in the gentle breeze. "Don't be afraid, *macane*. I'm always with you."

Alex sighed, certain the dead were just as devoted to you as you were to them. She finished the last sip of her *slivovitz* and headed back in the house.

"Bring out the good glasses, will you, honey?" asked Zvona, grinning as Jose rushed to the dining room.

"So, he knows where you keep your good china?" said Alex as she smacked her mother's bottom.

"He also knows to put the toilet seat down."

They both laughed.

"I'm really glad about you and Jose, Mom."

"Don't go reading too much into this. We're just dating, that's all."

"Well, the important thing is that he makes you smile," said Alex as she heard a car pull up in front of the house. Walking to the window, she saw Jason whistling as he came up the path, flowers in hand, his broad smile accenting the tiny wrinkles around his eyes. He adjusted his newly pressed shirt into his khaki pants and then knocked on the door.

"Hey, honey. I heard you were back," he said as he planted a big kiss on her cheek. "These are for your mother," he said as he handed Alex the bouquet.

"Are you feeling better?"

"Yeah, no worries. The shoulder's coming along nicely with the physical therapy and all. I should be back on the court within a month."

"That's really good news," said Alex as she stood awkwardly shuffling her feet. "Jason, listen, I'm really sorry I haven't called. Things have been pretty rough for me these last few days."

"I heard your visit registered pretty high on the Richter Scale," he told her, his eyes devilishly twinkling, challenging Alex to a verbal bout. "No wonder they name hurricanes after women."

Alex pursed her lips, holding back a smile and a rebuttal. "They changed that policy a while ago."

"Oh, did they? Too bad, it really made sense," he replied, eyeing Alex with a tenderness only reserved for her.

"You're pissed at me, aren't you?" she asked him as she slid her arm around his waist.

"Why because you left me to die on the sidewalk and ran off with some crazed assassin? Hell no!" he told her good-naturedly. "I'm not pissed, a bit bewildered, but then it's you."

"Thanks."

"Look, honey," he told her with a crafty wink. "I wouldn't take back a minute of the pain you've given me. Not a single minute."

"Is that a compliment?" Alex laughed, whole-heartedly.

"Call it what you will, but they not only broke the mold when they churned you out, they smashed it to pieces!" he announced with pride. "But, I wouldn't want it any other way. Nothing like having an original."

"You're a sucker for punishment," she said as he pressed his lips on her cheek.

"I guess that's what they call unconditional love," he said as he grabbed Alex's hand and directed her to the kitchen. "Let's go drink a toast to your Teta Maria."

"I couldn't think of a better way to start the evening," Alex agreed, as she felt her aunt's sacred presence fill the room.

She turned for a moment and looked out at the setting sun on the horizon. The wind blew gently in from the Atlantic, bringing with it the fresh salt air, and a message. The voices of the dead echoed in the branches, calling to her. *The path is yours, Alex, deviate not, be one of the righteous, for the world is sorely lacking of courage. Be one of the just few.*

"I will," Alex whispered back to the wind, lifting her glass in toast. She tossed the shot of slivovitz down her throat then headed for the living room, joining the others.

"Jose, do me a favor, will you?" she asked as she sank into the sectional couch facing her editor. "Call your buddy at the *London Times* and tell him I'll be calling about a job."

Jose smiled broadly as tears welled up in his eyes. "Can I at least finish my cocktail first, Alex?"

"Sure," she responded, her eyes wild with excitement. "Oh, and one other thing," she continued. "It's Alexandra from now on."

"You got it *mi amor*," replied Jose, lifting his glass in air. "To the future and to life."

"*Ziveli!*"

Endnotes

[1] www.jasenovac.org

[2] www.jasenovac.org

[3] www.jasenovac.org

[4] Glenny, Misha. The Fall of Yugoslavia.

[5] www.antiwar.com, BalkanExpress, Nebojsa Malic.

[6] Andras Riedlmayer, Aga Khan Program for Islamic Architecture, The Bosnian Manuscript Ingathering Project, Fine Arts Library, Harvard University.

[7] www.antiwar.com, BalkanExpress, Nebojsa Malic.

[8] www.antiwar.com, BalkanExpress, Nebojsa Malic.

[9] Shackelford, Michael. The Black Hand, The Secret Serbian Terrorist Society. University of Kansas, www.raven.cc.ukans.edu

[10] Shackelford, Michael. The Black Hand, The Secret Serbian Terrorist Society. University of Kansas, www.raven.cc.ukans.edu

Printed in the United States
18381LVS00004B/363